loving
without
being
vulnrabul

hi

allth best

luv bill

bill bissett

talonbooks

Copyright © 1997 bill bissett

Published with the assistance of The Canada Council

Talonbooks
#104—3100 Production Way
Burnaby, British Columbia
Canada V5A 4R4

Typeset in Adobe Caslon. Printed and bound in Canada by Hignell Printing Ltd.

First Printing: September 1997

pomes previouslee apeerd in 1) *take out* (portland oregon) 2) *carnival* (toronto canada)
3) *corridors* (montreal quebec) 4) *collision* (new bedford MA) 5) *literary and performance scenes*
(toronto ontario) 6) *descant 97* (toronto, ontario) 7) *queen street quarterly* (toronto,ontario)
8) *canadian journal of contemporary literary stuff* (toronto, ontario)
All drawings in *loving without being vulnrabul* are by bill bissett and many of these drawings are
from the collections of Jonathan Rainbow and Michel Potvin and of Catherine Yule.

Talonbooks are distributed in Canada by General Distribution Services,
30 Lesmill Road, Don Mills, Ontario, Canada, M3B 2T6; Telephone: (416) 445-3333;
Fax: (416) 445-5967.

Talonbooks are distributed in the U. S. A. by General Distribution Services Inc.,
85 Rock River Drive, Suite 202, Buffalo, New York, U.S.A., 14207-2170;
toll-free Telephone: 1-800-805-1083; Fax: 1-800-481-6207.

Canadian Cataloguing in Publication Data
Bissett, Bill, 1939-
Loving without being vulnrabul

Poems.
ISBN 0-88922-372-6

I. Title.
PS8503.I78L68 1997   C811'.54   C97-910725-3
PR9199.3.B45L68 1997

letting go uv our kodependenseez
our komplex with holdinga

i was driving in 2 hundrid mile hous in th karibu northern bc

n saw big sign on th left   sd

ANIMAL HOSPITAL   thot 2

myself well thers nothing reelee

wrong with me now   but if i take

anee turn 4 th wors   i cud go in

2 see doktor racoon   or nurs squirrel

its reassuring 2 know thers help

sew close by   well wud yu go

in2 a building sd PEOPUL HOSPITAL

iuv bin with peopul

loving   without   being   vulnrabul

manee timez
i *was* considring th wayze uv sunnee
n murkee possibiliteez   yet ther was is ar
onlee th wayze that can happn he sd as i was
am accepting ths evreething opend up 2 b
sew much eazier yes as iul nevr b as i was
onlee th inkredibul non logikul un translatabul
wayze uv being as i am wun n multipul n
present within WHAT   GOWD th WATR N
SEE KREESHURS wer FLOODING thru
evn th closd windos thees opnings involv
not being pressurd he went on by anee othrs
my selvs or schedules accepting YES th
kontra dicksyuns embray sing th process sure
unknowing th goal like whats th point ok xcept
we b 2gethr   ar flying undr th giant looming sew
neer sew far sew manee manee ITS A NU GAL
AXEE   star flamingoes constellaysyun bneeth
th selestshul shaydee evr reeching branches
comets shooting hi liting go on suddn path wayze
luxuriating in th sensitiv breezes yes th ocean
ripping thru us in all direksyuns each wave n
us disapeering   now they see it is not how it is
if yr not vulnrabul how ar yu in love he askd
its a nu kind uv loving i sd n its reelee possibul
may b n is reelee mor wundrful whn it can happn
uv kours not always   me ium ths close 2 happee
ness i sd   yet th scene changes melting in anothr supr hot
spell whats th point uv lerning lessons   if we cant
remembr them
our specees skreemd in2 th deep turquois whale
nite teeth sew rippuling shine swet dripping off
them tusks prodding gnashing our legs off blood
spurting   s h a r k s   interrupting our picknick
ing   *or* us trappd in anothr ice age brrrrrr big
time *or caut in a suddn tidal wave*   its th big wun

8

fine   ride it   out   arint we   sew small
squishd undr all ths watr is it still calld
th atlanteek   or   burreed undr   an un
announsd erth quake ar they evr   ANNOUNSD
WHAT AR YU SAYING

dont give yr heart   unless
dont give yr heart   s h a r e   its a
dont give yr heart   transplant

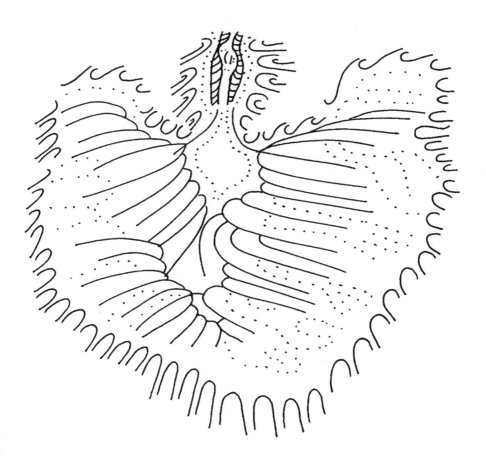

who has   seen   th defisit

our leedrs wudint tell us a storee a
ficksyun o
no   disgraceful potash sircumstances madam
cumstances apoth e oasis apothee cary went
wild evree time don was in 2 him psychikalee
or as th streem neembsee pretend various x
pektaysyuns arriving
th purpos uv th rhetorik
uv th ruling klasses is 2 make us pesants feel bad
evn guiltee not ourselvs
n our leedrs 2 knee jerk
cut n slash whn th i m f sz sew imf imf we watch
totalee objekting whil   our leedrs steel from th poor
n give 2 th rich
robert mcnamarra sd he was sorree
abt th war in vietnam that it had bin a mistake OOPS
th ovr 3 millyun killd   aftr that war he was appointid
ths was in reel life   wun uv th heds uv th i m f

in 20 or sew yeers will mcnamarra write anothr book
saying hes sorree abt busting th yuunyuns creating
a world wide undrklass as a result uv free trade global
restrukshuring deels n insistens on veree low key
soshul programs strip govrnment th pesants owe big
time leedrs veree rich cant owe as a result uv
poliseez uv i m f mcnamarra was 4 a time hed uv

th peopul returnd 2 themselvs she
carreed ths othr his hed wrappd in towels filld with
ths leedrs blood   th carriage going fastr n fastr back
2 th pastoral medow n appul tree places deep in
larkspur n raven song
th hot gold glaysing eye uv
th green n bountiful hill side   his hed singing ovr th
rich n deep   equalitee song blood all wayze running
on th post whn wud it dry his sew beautee hed
was resting nevr resting stuk on beeming

as we leev now th gods uv manee xcuses n burn our
skin on th freshlee erodid sun

let th watr sit 4 a day n th chloreen
evaporates

we livd on top uv a glass hill   wher evree
thing was alredee with us no seering need 2
serch th crevices uv th inside uv th startchd
stretchd purpul caverna dank full uv echoez
clattring suddnlee on th bronze stone luminous
in its chillee unfolding 4 watr suppliez projekts
possibiliteez or love without wch aftr all tho
th life uv th imaginaysyun nevr faltrs it can
go on un heedid by preskripsyun n evenshulee
    evree thing fails yet inbtween thos polariteez
    xtreems thers a lot uv life he sd we tuk a look
    outside it was inkrediblee dens th fog th swirl
    ing un known entiteez obviouslee shut off th
volume on th wide band announsr n maroond
ourselvs gentlee on th rockee ledg n waitid
    found among th flowrs wer items uv all our
    dreems n sighing   its veree beautiful by th
    see side drinking xcellent koffee by th fresh
ocean spray uv kours its sumtimes rockee
changing agendas n rhythms eye dont
assess it seulment   support it whatevr
    its all 4 lerning   acceptans n watching th
    big waves change '... hi its veree lovlee
        by th see side   at last finding pees n con
        tentment in xcellent companee n th waves
        ar sew tall n th koffee sew fabulous we feel
we cud bathe in th sunshine   well past infin
    itee..' i got my sunnee opia thru wun uv my
travls thru southern centralia now ium laffing
by th see shore spinning storeez uv motivaysyun
n othr peopul with a close frend theereez uv
relaysyunships its wundrful by th seeside sew
warm n magikul n we laffd at th daring lines

uv th lyrik from th old song *green slimee wishes*
'...hes an xploding gazoleen tank a sharpnel
cutee...'

now at last we cud laff at almost aneething

health hazzards

up north   peopul still talk abt it   what happend

evn if kustomrs wud komplain abt her koffing in 2
th food she was cooking 4 us all   konstantlee chain
smoking   ashes n phlegm dropping in 2 th hamburgr
stek   whatevr   n evree wun getting sick espeshulee
if she wer sick alredee   she wud say   ths is my
restaurant if yu dont like it   thers anothr kafay
onlee 20 miles away   they wer miles thn

aftr a numbr uv yeers she acquired such terribul
emphaseema she had bcum way 2 sick 2 run th place
all th time her grown son had parshulee takn ovr
but whn she was well enuff 2 work th place she was
back in   cooking n koffing smoking n serving
wheezing n hacking   choking n puffing   all ovr th
grill th food n us

we wer all reelee sorree she was oftn sick n mor
sorree whn she was 2 sick 2 work but thos times
whn she wud b totalee layd up gave us all a repreev
a short spell uv possibul wellness we cud almost
look 4ward 2 if it wer not always connektid 2 th
fact she wud b sick

2 sick 2 run a restaurant anee mor   she n her son
sold it n moovd 2 a trailr park   her trailr was wired
totalee 4 oxygen   evn in 40 below sheud go out in
th deep snow 4 a smoke   sumtimes ths got 2 her
not surprizing   considring th kold n th bothr
uv getting dressd in layrs 2 go out 4 it suck it
in sigh it in deep all th khemikuls tobakko nik
oteen   smoke n th hacking koffing wud start up
agen   she cud nevr smoke konstantlee whil watch
ing teevee anee mor   or nevr aneemor smoke inside
th trailr   nevr anee mor can b veree hard

wun day she had had enuff   ium told   her son had
gone away   n was cumming home 2 see her   not 2 far
from th trailr court   he cud see his mothrs trailr   had
she sd   ta hell with it   it had bin building up 4 a coupul
wintrs now   she wantid a cigarett   without th total
xasperaysyun   uv going out in   at that time 25 below
th whol big deel   she wud oftn komplain abt   ium told
well i had herd in th kafay   her konstantlee komplain
ing   n she had a kind heart   giving peopul credit
stuff like that

she lit th last cigarett   in her own trailr   sat down 2
watch a soap on teevee   n b4 her son cud reech th
trailr   it all went   KABOOM   giant thundring bomb
that was herd 4 kilometrs   shook th whol trailr court

her son was shockd n freekd   seeing all ths KABOOM
in th sky   n siteing   peesus uv his mothrs life   dispers
ing   ovr th icee landscape

in a klinik down south   th son restid 4 a whil   he was
a kind prson 2   kind peopul have diffikulteez   as he
got bettr   ium told   he decidid   his mothr ovr 75 at
that time   sure we can go on   a lot longr thn that   but
evn a few seconds uv a gud smoke   in front uv th teevee

n wintr safelee   n beautifulee   outside   brite sunshine
glinting off   th ice n snow   lovlee day   wud b worth
it   n it was   i gess   aftr all   her call

15

barometer basement turbines

yes baybee oh yes ths is sew wundrful
eye love it whn yu dew that treets me like
sugar whn ium reelee a walking mattress
well maybe i am kind uv sugar or a cedar tree
or an offis dreem i want out uv ths
plant ium 2 close 2 th hydranjas not
that th lilaks arint eezee enuff 2 get
along with cheree have yu got a twentee
just 4 a week or sew okay thanks i love
yu gotta go cum a croppr tales uv such
wundr he uv kours george saild his watree
thots out 2 th reef wher he herd th maidens
singing ther until his heart meltid n he was
abul 2 get back 2 shore n give n listn n
emptee 4 a whil n enjoy frequent melting
xcellent he sd th maidens wer
in great voises nowun els had
herd them no wun els such
need 2 as ned george buttrs th
name buttrs he oftn felt he cud dew
without oh if onlee he cud quit smoking
yes xercise mor swimming in th moon tides
star loft zeno wasint it th meteors wher
they had fell 2 erth he kept massaging his
cheek against teers uv awesumness glay
zing th emeralds on th stone in
layd ther 4 centureez n th whiskr
breth being uv th doorway cutikul
chopin n snow kastuls leening on th
marmaduke inlet th cawsyunaree sun rise
n th morning birds spitting crows n swallows
n gulls lifting th huge konkreet towrs n lovrs
carreeing them away n dropping them
out 2 see   heers wher th note

16

endid reed eye add n endangerd th mor
reeding uv with th suddn flapping uv th
traktor home is wher th n o barnyard
villa o bettr late thn n th doors what
dew yu call them doors in th floors th
cellar doors no hurricane *tornado*
doors no well they wer flapping opn n
shut opn n shut th huge wind
was cumming from bneeth
them thos un nameabul
doors n i was out uv ther
skrambling with ths parchment
tuckd undr my arms thats it
trap doors
snap my fingrs oh
silvr green spires n goldn tempul
towrs
gees n sheep flying ovr th
trembling third from th left
zounds balustrade not weeping in
sarrous n tree time citeez
writtn in th sand evree
thing is   onlee 2 un
covr onlee 2 reecovr save save
th gestyur n th artikulating   mandribul
n genius   echoez n
sparkling lettrs in   th sand
spelling out th natural events
n th bonding changes n th brindling
bodee   n levitating ecstaseez n th
sources uv th origins we sigh n
die 4 tongues uv th origins we
lovinglee whispr 4   it is that glade
lokatid in that undrwatr deepness
wher th vial uv undrstandings   rests
we onlee need 2 swim 4   not 2 shore far
undr n th watr greets us n kisses

us inside our heds n eyez n hearts n
soul   n we leep in 2 th ocean
floor   tides n merkor   see th orange
beem   sleep blu thru   ths
big wet   kashanee
pulling us in
side its 4
evr pulsing
kiss

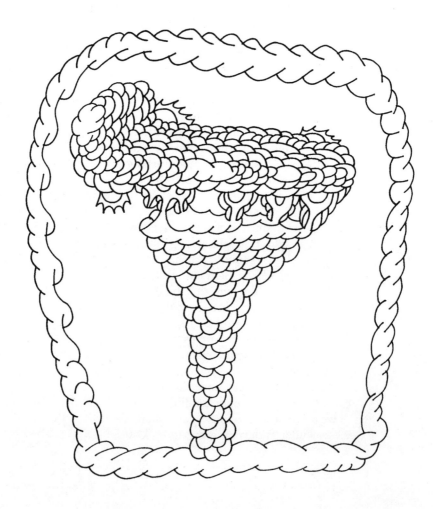

whn yu walk in 2 th room
n yr waiting 4 me
n all is gladness n lafftr
o cum n see

n we put our arms around each othr
n glide on in 2 th stars

n we dont care aneemor yu know whethr
theyr calld venus or mercuree or
mars

we go 2 th northern lites n th fires
n th dreems protekt our souls n magik rabits
n kiyots dansing around our love
n we go gliding in 2 th stars n we dont care aneemor
yu know whethr theyr calld venus or mercuree or
mars

n we go gliding in 2 th stars
n we go gliding in 2 th stars
n we go gliding in 2 th stars

ths is how it cud b she sd 2 me

god or th goddess as yu like 2 say is a giant
child   leening against a giant window sill
looking out at rolling emerald hills th shining
turquois watr brite yello zaneeness birds evree
wher   lifting melodeez

we peopul us human beings our world turning
yes our galaxee   lives inside a tiny dust ball or
bowl on th bottom sill sumtimes she he is sew
fascinatid with us   th giant child has amazing
vishyun or eye site   n watches us swarming
like ants robots now 2 th left thn th xtreem
rite killing each othr 4 nothing   th smart talk
will go on as she he tells th othrs abt us seez
us yakking on tiny teeveez 2 xplain evreething
bunduling up 2gethr kissing   inside huge gold
flowrs

they thats us rush ths way thn that as if
answring importantlee sum innr loud speekr
pendulum like   sew oftn group behaviour its
weird disgusting she he sz 2 her his great con
fidents uv othr giant childrn n adults all loom
ing sew tall ovr us   observing our tantra n
lassitudes xtreem organizaysyuns   whers th
prson in it all   rare n hard 2 find

sumwuns at th door   she he th giant child turns
2 answr it his her elbow sleev brushes against
us   we ar all turnd ovr hurtuling in 2 xploding
in 2   s p a c e   tumbuling ovr n ovr is it a
dryer   4evr spinning no not xactlee tidal waves
land slides volkanik erupsyuns also occur from
ths clothing arm brushing past us rocks watr
fill our lungs crack our heds skreeming we ar
limp tiny dolls falling thru th shatterd ceilings
uv our owning brains owwwww

certain mor auspisyus membrs uv ths prartikular
giant familee   perhaps mor euridite thn othrs ar
reeding   whil thees diastrs wreck our   specees
theyr current nu age best sellr   *th benign univers*

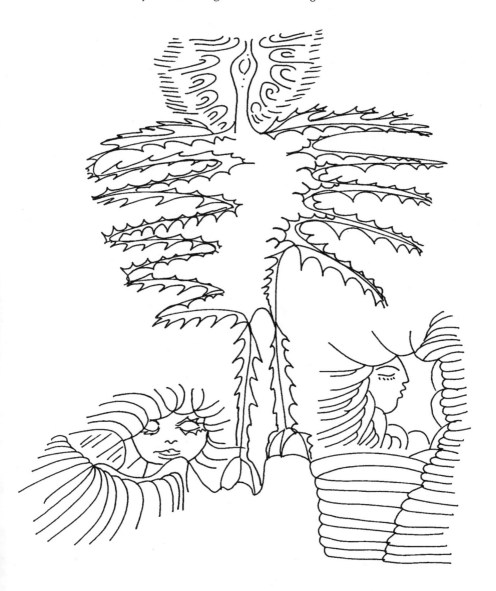

evree thing was fine until they startid shoot
ing   evreewun

whoaaaaaaaaaaaaaaaaaaaaaaaaaaaaa

a field calld iago   th othr parenting   suspisyus
         paranoid self   saying   wher yu ar
is no gud 4 yu   th critikul self rathr

have yu evr herd a field talking

yes i have i sd   ther ar fireweed n baybeez breth
   growing out uv th hills   broom wild berreez hayze
      uv th sun on th birds   sparrows barn swallows
humming birds   n th beez flying in n out uv th
flowrs th lake evn mooving in th blurring mirage
uv th breezes n wind   changing evree thinking a
lot uv commenting   carreez on

   what i wantid 2 dew with a big bowl uv klam
   chowdr   or no corn chowdr   with sum rye bred
      toast   looking ovr th kokahalla

or

thers a big sigh on th phone   ths can b ironee or

a guilt manoeuvr   or a wrong numbr   iul say

   illusyuns   washing all th cupbords   ther was

a dairee farm i wud go 2   they spoke in tongues
ther a lot uv raging hurricanes cud always b
arriving   taking evreething away th crops cud
   always turn out no gud   peopul broke u up
   sumtimes with theyr changing n partnrs n

evreething els   uv kours evn whn times wer
    gud   they tried 2 teech themselvs   its all part
uv th dansing thredding greeving laffing letting
go   not trying 2 fix things   2 allow   all part uv

th dansing   sumtimes peopul wud get up tite
    cudint let go uv theyr memoreez   attachments

2 th fire   as they saw it   n thn

a hurricane was nothing

23

lookit th pickshurs uv yr self

takn 15 yeers ago   th face is
almost unrecognizabul   th mind also has bin
replaysd manee timez

yu want 2 say th minds
th same   yet is ther a same   n in replaysing
ther is replenishing

cud we b whol   like a grain
field bfor harvesting   isint it all   process
onlee   wher is th freez frame   or

anee capturing uv image port
abul bfor carving imprintid in th fluid   cells
uv our brain   how we act   evn is

sew   changing ahhh   attachment   n th nausea

hed rest phones   bulletin bords   flexibiliteez

th hungree soul 4 certaintee   sure is a   hot wun
he sd   picking me up n takn me farthr along
th road
colors uv stamina   n optimism evree
thing changes th   fethrs we   weer   starting out
agen   yr kinda young lookin 2 b out on ths road
ths time uv nite   by yrself   he sd 2 me   ·

sure is wet he sd pickin me up by th gulch   dont
usualee see guys   middul age like yu he sd out
hitchin   whirling in th wind   n th moistyur

montage sequens uv pick ups   wher did th yeers uv
travelling begin   2 put it ther   pin point th
needul in th   our fingrs touching as we ar

passing   th glass btween   our compatibul beings

fire   erth

a day uv sun moon   stars   sew far away them
selvs   glowing   th memoreez uv our previous
lives   we carree   with us   in 2 th simmring
        phases   uv what   we dont know   it
all wayze turns out or oftn   tho we know sew
hard we hurt ourselvs   fine it mostlee changes
   bfor we can grayze   its suddn n resilient
messages   fly off us

e tuk off his hat   she sat down in2 th
   flowring   ground   wher sparrows had bin
                    swimming   in th sky

n he sd 2 him   look i dont know   i cud wait
til   sum wun passes by

or letting go uv th stanse   onlee   th rumors uv
           immortalitee   sustain us   or regardless
        uv that   what i want 2 focus on my self
                                                    selvs

it happns ovr n ovr agen xcellent   until th
   appetite changes oh   i dont know i sd its
   evreething els   peopul getting brutal n th virus
thats whats changing all that 4 me   now evn 2
   protekt myself from disapointment eye dont
   hope   its a plateau   a harmone colliding with
uv kours poetenshul opnness 2 sumthing happning
sum wher els   its a veree spiritual phase reelee with
a lot uv greef 4 all individuals evree wher no wun
is immune from   th changing privaseez n ownr
ships uv emosyuns dont n dew interest me sail
ing   n grounding n arint we   all each day left
with our own intrpretaysyuns   uv our own lives

evasiv   deskriptiv   passages   n ths   fleeting

            boiling   time

among th arbutus in th coastal area

n th tanguld tangoed awakenings she sd it dusint
mattr what they say we will almost all wayze ms mistr
intrepet them n them us bcoz ther is no direktness
sew fulfill yr selvs not asking is ths okay with yu sew
oftn how that is veree xcellent i sd 2 evreewun 2 em
brayse th unknown n blessings on th missd mistr
n deferrd connexsyuns

i tried 2 found a civilizaysyun in ths mirror building he
sd peopul skreeming dont reflekt me damn yu et
setera now ium letting go in th bird tree hous sending
frends on th main hi in th smoke undr th dansing
stars heer wher unknown lafftr n singing on th smok
ing porch treez huge n tendrilling grow all around us
inside us leep ovr us filling th inkee magnetik sky
watr evreewher evn drenching our dreems how dew yu
make changes in yr life accepting n thn or opposing
whatevr how much shifting can yu accept ther is no
place 4evr

sew at th deepest levl we blame othrs bcoz we think wer
alone n its theyr fault tho thers reelee no proof we ar
totalee alone if espeshulee we invoke th xistens n act
iviteez uv othr dimensyuns thos we cant reelee see is
that what yr saying yes ned sd hmmm i sd n mused
furthr sew sumtimes in a crowd uv peopul who know
us as ,,, we have indentitee 4 that n thats xcellent
n by ourselvs waiting 4 our lovr 2 call without seeming
2 ourselvs 2 b sew waiting working endlesslee on th
text is anothr identitee thees ar all aspekts uv what
eye want 2 manifest n undr lying our feers uv othrs
ko dependenseez on us is our own feer uv being alone
n having onlee th invisibul 4 companee not being dis
missiv ther not at all gud companee is always welcum

**whethr its visibul or not listning 2 each prsons storee
is sew interesting helpful as we accept as we wrestul**
with thees demons uv our own minding letting go uv our own ko
dependenseez wch if we give up we may xperiens mor changing

identiteez not 2 worree o gram mateeka eye cant see yr teeth go
eezee on th teeth or yu can b ruff with yr teeth a bit dont hold
back swimming goez onlee from dawn 2 dusk our feers what
dew they help us with not much not enjoying survival neon
n haddock cod n lily pools sumtimez its not sew much chang
ing identiteez 2 say that as being flexibul with what we have
not xpekting evreething 2 go our way accepting our own core
diversiteez i was undrstanding my self s 2 well mesuring th invi
taysyuns 4get that

aneeway arriving at my own discovereez jewels uv undrstanding
in all ths moistyur th jewels shine as my undrstanding s dew i
was journee 2 see a familee membr gone ths far 4 yet not possibul
disapointment acceptans acceptans we try 2 take care uv each
othr ideelee our specees whn thats wantid n th soshul network
guaranteez 4 evreewun must b in place or we bcum look hopeless
lee brutal hand yes give a touching th sereen empteeness n full
ness we ar inhabit reelee he hugs me on th radioway all th lites
uv th carnival spreding in our minds on th freeway park gardening
th gates uv th moon lit nite he walks away aftr disapeering vista
jauntee as th roadwayze melting   ium speeding ovr offis towrs sub
urb houses happning streets layzee nosee slumbring pinnakuls
uv bedrooms with all us toy peopul big feelings trying 2 undr
stand enuff uv undrstanding we nevr will time out from pleez
ing 2 go deepr we share ths 2gethr sub textualee if onlee th
sardeens manos wud i cud i meemo th way is now othr el
ementz presentaysyuns 4 prson soul being greeting not hurt
ing deepr ther n turning pleezes missd connexyuns kissing him
enjoy our own sleight uv hand anothr konstrukt ovr pass ovr
soul ovr nite ovr getting ovr evreething or standing ovr undr evn
he evn he fine i cud heer all th muskratz tendenseez see th
hook th needul in th sky knowing thers no wher 4 me 2 go but
heer with myself totalee wrapping around myself ths nite not
pleezing aneewun els prais or blame enjoying sigh ths non
agenda sleeping chill listn 2 th rain see th vishyun uv my
spirit guide my frend 2nite in th treez turning side wayze his
hed erring gold joining with me endlesslee 4 ths time wher
it also counts breething breething mirakul uv ths

greener pastyurs have helpd our specees
ovr millenia n millenia

4 ginny n alan

n seeing
            all th purpul starfish sucking breeth
ing hudduling ovr th rocks by th ocean in out in
  out with such loyaltee devotidlee guiding holding
th rocks from sliding splashing sinking in 2 th end
less watr   n i gess o us 2 n th
                        rock cliffs all uv us
  hi n dry from falling in
                  2 th big wet it was a bed 4
raptyur th loving song they wer silentlee singing
ths has helpd a lot 2 we ar grateful 4
                        in th footnotes
  we reflektid on our sumtimes acute capasitee 4 imagin
                        ing disastrs
how precarious our mind holding on 2 whatevr can b
  growing all th mor lowring 2 our remembring thos
cruelteez that had bin dun 2 us how we deel with
thos   tho thats not xactlee how we wantid 2 phrase
it as if sum tactilitee has gone washing out 2 see
  that awareness letting
                  th purpul color is sew great
n th wayze thees starfish entwine themselvs 4 kilometrs
along th shore smell th musculs load salt fasten in
  trikatelee theyr konstello
                  a theyr star tentakuls
des étôiles round th always 2 shifting shore les étôiles
  de mer singing theyr songs uv mareen attach
ment
        if we hold yu mould yu willl nevr scold yu yu
  wunt moov o sensual singing breethings toads
                      springing duck
         ing th spray blu herons bask in th
  mouldee clay slate rocks 4 lasting pedestal yu
from anee slipping falling sliding subtul
        changings recordings th millenia
            n millenia

ps i beleev in communitee he sd   evn in spirit
watching ovr me   letting th baggage go nu co
ordinates   grinding down on th geers   a big shift
                                    cumming

well   heer in th an othr alitee   we watch nite long
ovr th purpul   star fish   soft pedes   th land sighing
singing   th

                    harold th moon beem child   also saw 2
all ths   th cumming n   going n   moistyur murmur
ings uv all thees
                    th starree   crustaysyun plan now
opn nu frends wer mooving in 2 my hed brain see
ing th space 4 lees sign above th oral surgeree
    doktor kuff bringing theyr own fetal tissu   n
    enuff xtra 4 me i cud use sum give an addid
briteness   freshness   2 each nu day
                                    i love yu harold
                sd 2 les étôiles de mer   yu signal me
                        my gills n un reesonings my
                    thrills   n back door pockits   my
        yernings n fansee sausage   i will always
                    will yu   approaching
th door n th harmoneez   n th ears travl servis
whnevr eye call   n make my arrangementz   sun uv
sand papier   glassee terrain we slithr ovr glistn
    ing   call back   returning th wheel we danse
                    on with 2gethr sew manee
                    othr flying buses n larch treez   nu
        zeeland appuls   onlee blessings
                                onlee blessings
                    onlee blessings

a gathring uv smallr koffs fresh in from scotland
looking mor melancholee thn   n smallr thn   usual
was assembled on a farthhr rock ledging   discuss
    ing th inevitabul sadness th turning in theyr
        necks   funereal sew like buzzards

29

n th purpul starfish continuing
2 brace th land   from th see   holding all   our
homez in place   from th big washing   ovr

it was a bed 4 raptyur   th song   we all   wer
singing   dansing   raptyur   scents   uv melon
see   spray   cold   rock   spreding   n pastyur
gayzing

whn last we bridgd narrow refrunks
doktor 2day

skin pebbuld by th salt spray heetid by th o zoneless
sun tho heo theo rio o o leo me neo pia zio
  thereo thereoareamio veto vio vio zio loz in

th blanketing comforting darkness n slowlee upon
each rabbit n hunting kiyot th foxes in theyr bundul
dreem each flowr upon n th dogs erupti barking at
evree echoed breething no mattr how silent at th
6th dimensyun uv mystikul sun rooms n stiltid offis
towrs th intensyun or wind whispr n it will taste
  around th buick comet langwage wantid th braid
ing lariat n who languishd in th vitriol eyelids sunee
mending was th third or fifth 2 cum thru th drama
  bursting uv july doorbells in th hearts roasting
our toez on th seement hau hsu tsu sun t sting
taybul what is th lingring languor u ask cud it b in
th treez cud it b inside yr chest th coppr windos
gleeming
              eye pulld th zippr all th way heeld th
heart pulld it out 4 sum air an unheraldid commiss
aree was set up 2 teer th pilots a lot got shreddid oh
  a must see proprtee in kluding th view sun sets sun
risis th like uv wch see monstr lavishing borrowing
tone cum in 2 our dreems our vexaysyuns sereen mo
ments rising from th toxik dumps undr th school yards
    th childrn teechrs brain cansers
                                  no thank yu in
th surprizing snow cougar walleeing a round th front
door keep it closd feel th magik out ther th hungr n
th hot breth storms favorit staysyuns ar eradikatid wires
down in th fridg look 4 blessings ooo ice kreem in th
neighbours buttrflies
                    as huge as our WISHES in erlee
spring apeer carrees softn covr us in theyr flapping n
softlee talking lakes brush th teers n rips from our
face tho they dont lessen th vishyun uv th bull dozrs
    n th masheen guns on th brite horizon

jean marc   did i evr tell yu

abt th time i was in
a circus   i lookd aftr th elephants n i desired
th hed acrobat   he tuk me in 2 his bed manee
timez   our affair lastid elevn countreez   th
circus travelld thru south amerika north
amerika   all uv europe afrika china
india   he showd me sum uv his triks
on th hi wire with his hi flying act
sumtimes sew 2gethr it was we wer spinning
btween th sun n th moon   n all th stars
whn i look up at them at nite uv cours
i think uv thos times n see us agen   up
ther   aloft with or without th roar uv
th gaping audiens   we wer entring th
biggest smiles uv th world theyr mouths
opning letting us in   in 2 rivrs uv glotis
n all along theyr manee tonsils yet sew
suspendid   in theyr awaiting arms n
his hands around me aftr 4giving me 4
anee uv th slips i may have made n
praising me with his eyez n fingrs 4
my sumtimes agilitee

we seldom travelld
by train usualee in trucks n wagons sum uv us
evn walking 4 spells 2 get air let our heds out in
2 th outtr sky n clouds n galaxee   feel our own
bodeez 4 a whil apart from th collektiv uv
all uv us performrs i had joind th act now we
uv cours wud want 2 re gathr   cud nevr live
without 4 veree long   each othr yr getting
sleepee a bit no well wun time we tuk th train

it was barrelling along full spit   hot steem evree

wher so much whn we wud rush thru
suddn tunnuls apeering th windows wud b
quite coverd   as if mor is going on in life thn
reelee is   n thn thos hours n hours undr th
        burning autumn moon across th prairee uv
wher evr we wer thn   haunting n abjektlee in
trospektiv i was feeling as if sumthing wer abt 2
happn not in th act   we stoppd sumwher outside uv
odessa we all got out it was veree cold our brite
colord costumes onlee warming us in th midnite
attik uv sumwuns nite heer was it th middul uv
whos was it
                        whn we got on bord ther was a nu
animal trainr with us he was ruggid n carreed uv
cours his own whips mor trustworthee i herd
        sum wun had told me thn borrowing thos uv
th shows   whn his eyez met my acrobats my
    spirits sank ths nite was going 2 b at worst a
threesum i cudint beleev it we had just gottn
reelee 2gethr my acrobat n me   ths was a difficult
passage dimitri my acrobat left our bunk aftr in th
    erlee morning iul see yu latr pierre he sd dont
moan abt ths
                        my hed ache worsend as th train
hurld itself thru th vastness   dimitri returnd
    well aftr th brekfast time i had had no stomach
    4 i had nevr thot myself immortal th anxietee
uv being in a coupul ths was my first nite 4 that
n i almost willd my own deth bcos uv th absens
uv my lovr dimitri came back bleeding koffing
at leest not blood it was not th tb that was spreding
evreewher his back was bleeding ther wer welts
    on his arms n legs his red eyes wer rimmd
with teers as he crawld a woundid dog in bside
me n held me 4 his craving i submittid 2 him
    my hed cracking n my heart n psyche sew
wrackd with insecuriteez i just wantid 2
know what it felt like he sd

what it felt like 4 him was beetn his feelings
bcum totalee ritualizd wun   or th othr   top or
  bottom tho he had found sum part uv his soul
he sd he had not xperiensd bfor   i tried not 2 b
2 monogomous abt it b sharing accepting tho
as young as i was i went aftr lunch 4 ths intrudr
  upon my happeeness   it was not jealousee it
  was angr proteksyun uv my frend our life
2gethr

            he was beeting th animals unmersifulee
whn i came upon him with th axe n smashd him
down 4 all that he had betrayd in me tho we
  reelee hadint met   it didint take long th train
running thru mountains now i fed him 2 th
lions th stench was unbeerabul

                     in court whn
we finalee stoppd sumwher   th town we wer play
ing in i sd i tried 2 stop th lions from killing him n
  barelee escaped with my own life ther wer teers
  in my eyez uv cours no charges wer brout
against me   it was sd i was way 2 slite 2 have
  injurd sumwun as strong n burlee as th animal
trainr

            ahh that was a long time ago   ium not
sew slite now   well me n dimitri livd ovr 5 yeers
2gethr travelld thru ovr elevn countrees our
  love flourishd thru   iuv nevr felt total innosens
4 long evr sins that nite i killd th animal trainr
  well he almost killd my lovr   n sins th nite
  sevn yeers aftr that dimitri fell from th hi wire
a nite with no net   n all th audiens blood gush
  ing from its mouths like vomit skreeming n
  skreeming fell into th hard ground n saw dust
i wud stare in2 th moon   th sun th candul anee
fire in th erratik bleekness uv all my lost
  purpose sumtimes i wud feel him talking with
  me saying mor ths way mor that n whats

it like getting oldr   can yu find evr anee
wun els like me   now yr settuld in montreal
th moon looming sew hugelee ovr mont
royal have yu evr crawld up th steps 2 th top
ther uv th shrine   have yu found love like
yu evr lovd me

jean marc   cum 2 bed yu
miss sumthing 2nite yu alredee have evreething
ium with yu ths is th coldest nite uv th
yeer   th fire is still going in our hearts our
eyez 2morro iul tell yu anothr storee   no
yu want 2 wait   a day or so   a yeer or so a
dreem or sew yu know i am with yu 4
as long as it is ths journee   that was
a long time ago dont think uv it   cum
heer let me moov inside
yu

we ar strangr thn shellfish

soft belleez   ueueue   we protekt ourselvs bfor
aneething happns   try sew hard   not 2 sting first
we just want love   n cant find it   n we maybe disapeer
aftr ths 80 or whatevr watt bulb goez out   ay ther was
a shellfish   evolushyunaree role modeling sum times
peopul want 2 b alone   that gets skaree   thn we ar
with sum wun 2 much   gets weird   great at first
descend in 2 care taking   co dependenseez each
taking on th othrs feers   not living theyr own life
klawstrophobik ickee   stinging may ensue not letting
go uv obsessiv memoreez baggage   arbitraree
pestring we dont know our origins our needs we want
2 b left alone hurt alredee passing on mor changes

thn we cant stand being alone   its not novel or re
freshing aneemor how manee lives dew we have is
int it alredee 2 much off 2 merge files raging live 2
gethr agen evn tho we can love ourselvs   th child in
us is fine no mattr how multipul   our selvs ar n thats
a lot 2 love   how can we xpekt aneewun els 2 track all
that 4 us hang in with each othr see th nite sky
howling 2gethr n th morning   nevr seen b4 sun lite
n entransing we kiss our koffee kups n laydels

can we keep seeing eye 2 eye wher is th bizness what
plesyur our dreems bcum thredbare lacking paranoid
we totalee disagree on th tablow havint we dun ths b
4 is ths a layr mask 4 feer uv th othr leeving us can
we dew ths agen   raging out gonna find gonna find
its in th serching not th finding picasso sd   we get
involvd with peopul who ar dominating   they moov on
sum wun els seez us as mooving on no blame th mew
sik changes n th dansing n th compewtr skreen n th
humiditee   not alwayze sew grayshus wer luckee if wer
luckee ar all words circular nu versyuns uv old nu end
less cyculs undrstood by nowun   thers a missyun 4 yu
ms crustasyun blowing us kisses on late nite teevee talk

what othr specees has sd th son uv god had arrivd
on erth   amayzing wud jellee fish conjure ths whales
    dolphins delving in 2 ths much konstrukt trubul its
hit or myth   shellfish   dew they think uv gods dottr
    visiting among us prhaps cussins conveying our
grace sew much we sew far dont seem 2 get 2 know

    getting kleer 2day keep on spinning   humming
hemmings n hawings weird ths layring also ecstatik a
    long look long book wall uv lettrs sounds texts wher
did it start we look 4 places 2 b phrases 2 see n 2
    leev them thos leeving us nevr going   nests n up

heevals as i reech 4 yu agen strangr thn shellfish ar we
    n pleez each othr sew much agen n go no identitee 2
trap us confitur us until th longing rewrites us agen
    n we cum alive with each othr drinking n gorging
sew deep quenching n mooving on sum wun asks
    us 4 spare change dont we give not knowing ourselvs
how much change we have left scurree ing our wayz
    ovr th floor uv th sky

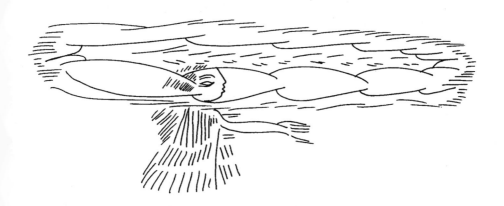

evreewuns talkin bout cut backs
   cut backs   th defisit th nu state religyun
   tax th poor mor   give 2 th rich

      evreewuns gettin cut sept th peopul
       on top o no   o yes   crueltee facade
  its th 2 byzanteen   snakes n laddrs
      evreewun whos promoting cuts is
       themselvs on top getting acceleratid
                              having highr wages

who dew we reelee owe aneeway isint
   th harranging by our leedrs th replace
   ment 4 original sin now that that
   doktrin has lukilee lost its lustr
   a rhetorik 2 make us all feel bad guilt us
   cut th arts poor eldrlee marginalizd mor
   whers th powr 2 fight back did bell canada
   pay taxes reed linda mcquaig   its all 4 free
       trade harmonizing with th empires retro
soshul system in ordr 4 our rulrs 2 b abul 2
   penetrate theyr market ther is a defisit but
       mostlee *thees cuts* will in canada give a
       tax brek 2 th rich n will onlee sumwhat
   dekrees th defisit sew its ideologikul n
                              manipulativ
       th nu lectur on us by th rulrs we r
   yes *us* ar spending 2 much on ourselvs
   with munee we cud claim is our own
   ths is not xcellent n regretfulee th rulrs
   will have 2 tax us mor   sew th balans
   can b addressd   they dont *want* 2   they
   wud love 2 tax big corporaysyuns n welthee
   peopul mor   but jobs wud dekrees evn
       mor unfortunatelee they must temporarilee

create mor unemployment by cutting back on
edukaysyun soshul spending health arts th
lies filtr down 2 us not th munee theyv takn
from us   our leedrs ar barking at us now they ar
veree frustratid by our inabilitee 2 get it   theyv bin
patient with us   soon they wunt have anee mor
time 2 xplain theyv got it yes us pesants wer we
2 beleev our leedrs wud feel guiltee flawd wher
can we go but down   its th trickul up effekt
can canada have th courage 2 b itselvs   no poor
cud top doktors salareez top hydro offishuls top
lawyrs top investors kanadian air bus lobbeeists b
cut or taxd mor   no not reelee oh well
cud we inkrees taxes on banks   wch ths yeer have
made theyr biggest profits evr   no not a gud moov
a lot uv 2 manee problems in all thees cases
our representativs xplain   we try 2 duck th big
                                        xplain
amazinglee banks ar nevrthless reseeving
grants from th govrnment   sumtimes seen as
    our tax dollrs   4 reserch n technolojee veree
    important n always dun   they xplain mor
a bank is not a hospital no
a bank is not a soshul program   veils uv
a bank is not free edukaysyun   th rhetorik uv
a bank is not an arts council   th rulrs they ar
a bank is not a bustid yunyuun   xperts on kontra
                                            diktoree soshul
is a bank a bizness   messag
all th leedrs ar talking bout   cut backs cut
    backs   returning us 2 suffring brutaliteez
    arts programs return 10 times 2 th ekonomeez
dew th peopul reelee owe   we build bridges
    isint it th leedrs who owe   with our taxes why
    is it likelee theyul pay us back   not art health edu
    its th rest uv us whoul pay   kaysyun thees ar
                                        bridges 2 our selvs

we ar part uv that tradishyun   pesants
gettin screwd by th rulrs   without plesyur

down down they want us   kolonizing us in
our own places homes schools

cud corporaysyuns pay reel taxes like us well no
that wud b naive
manee corporaysyuns
pay no reel taxes
a corporaysyun is not a womens half way hous no
cuts can happn ther not a street peopuls program
not oxygen 4 poor terminalee ill peopul at home a
corporaysyun is not an employee not a sheltr 4
batterd women not a down town hospital not gud
nutritsyun 4 poor childrn sew they can lern in
school   did mcmillan blowdell pay reel taxes
see linda mcquaig   whers th tax reform whers th
continuing path tord equalitee   th common
wealth wch munee is it is not reelee solee an
individuals thats a ideologikul storee 2 justify
2 rashunalize if us potenshul consumrs ar
totalee poor how can we buy thees moovs by
th rulrs will evn destroy themselvs will they
leev us just enuff 2 buy what they ar selling
us wch wud b th onlee produkts we can buy
duz canada have 2 imitate th empire th yew s

free market free market   dew yu beleev ontario
n alberta ar demokratikalee elektid govrnments
free market free market user feez eye feel
sew used dont yu werent health n edukaysyun
food sheltr clothing werent thees rites theyv
bin redefind as luxureez   dew yu beleev th huge
profits 4 bizness trade surpluses now that sew
manee yuunyuns ar bustid faktorees in th
south ahh yes individual initiativ eye made

40

all ths munee myself eye dont need thees workrs
  if i gave them mor they wud waste it thees
mytholojeez uv xcessiv rewards ar self corrupting
not self enobling   we pesants can watch thees
  arketypal tablows ahhh yes th familee figurs
tho unfortunalee as povrtee inkreeses battering
  all kinds uv domestik abuse n publik crime will
inkrees th top ideolojee will keep up with ths n
    comik strip blame a changing charaktr we can
  follow ths as it changes th storee wch will b
cum mor n mor brutal mor n mor cruel uv kours
    4 no purpos xcept 2 make thos on top mor n
  mor welthee tho sum sinseerlee beleev in th
top ideolojee n will b hideouslee confusd n them
  selvs guiltee tho will try 2 weer th rightyus mask
  4 as long as they can   engage in th seremonial
  dramas   at leest until debate is bannd

top peopul dont reed his her storee books 2 see
  what has happend bfor whn thees forces wer un
leeshd top peopul ar 2 bizee top peopul have a
  job 2 dew   4 our own gud   we can observ with
  no plesyur   we ar agen part uv that tradishyun
guaranteed minimum inkums 4 evreewun cud eez
thees sorree n ridikulus stricksyurs tragedeez
evreewun cud ern above that life duz not have
  2 b in anee way punitiv full uv pressurs feers
why b part uv th tradishyun   getting screwd with
ar we part uv that tradisyun   no plesyur

                        can we change it   will peopul
onlee remembr why we creatid a societee with in
kreesinglee fair soshul programs edukaysyun n
health 4 evreewun whn condishyuns ar sew

brutal they will see th reesons 4 th common welth

agen whers th change

LINGUISTIK MEWSIK

marianne moore sd '. . . poetree is reel
toads in imaginaree gardns ...'

thers allwayze sumwun bside us looking
out 4 us   dew yu feel th prson just ovr our
shouldr   bringing us candee at th brekwatr
luvlee dreems at th nite tide   as we ar poly
lecktik theree is a territoree she sd   yes i sd its
also th proteksyun 4 us from th binaree 2 faced
onlee oppressyun uv thos peopul who want
sameness or dominans ovr us our diffrences
from them they think themselvs universal
maxa majoray desirabul destabilizes thretns
them whn ther is no stabilitee n that reelee making
it thn mor possibul 2 *arriv* thru equalitee n mor
acceptances uv infinit multiplisiteez we need ar
manee kulturs 2 get thru evn wun life is manee
ecstatik juggulars we ar   perpetual   flowing
spinning   ar x changabul konstrrukts in th un
knowing air can b sew manee offrings wayze
brain waves b r a i n   w a v e s rain aves in
ra ar bran ran an na vesa save sa ve vase av
ban nAb NAR an rn bin bir bia ai bain naib
vesa wev wes was saw wave avew vew ewa

peopul ar oftn veree shy n tremulous not onlee
insecuriteez brout abt by unkind fate s   sew sel
dome can ther b reelee anee blame in romances
if wer responsibul 4 ourselvs th accidents uv
changing desire oftn sew sir madam reel prat
falls sorrow crying until ther isint anee mor n
ending what gardn s we can find ar present 2 us
consolé des étôiles always ther thredding lets
bundul up o tuna fishes wer animating with
scarves n leotards undr our outtr clothing yeh
well if yr getting it all day fine looking out ovr
th siberian infinit fields uv snow by th time

that prson gets 2 th glass   heul look thru it
see mor snow   i am th projeckyunist   no amount
uv mental xplaining can help   awe   avey   nair
we in theyr need 4 itself   alredee in us   th un ser
taintee   will it b met   can they ask 4   what they
need 2 keep going   2 th well   2 draw   th gud n
requird watr   embraysing th   blessing th contra
dicksyuns   territoree is also evasyun   he sd   eaves
on th moto   mooving thru th entangulmentz
eva i sd was lifting th countr   stepping thru n
greeting us   thn   giving us bon voyage as we set
sail   tuk off   disembarkd   leeving returning   avis
latin 4 th internal vishyun   cums n goez   n facts
can narrow   our xpektaysyuns   wch well we drink
from   not 2 hit on wun scenario onlee   th manee
ness uv storeez   simultaneouslee   xpressing   b
ing   n how oftn   not onlee tremulous in theyr
beering   theyr wanting love   peopul can evn
show angr   she sd   stormee in th northern seez
2 covr that   th erasyur   uv being 2gethr   th chang
ing road itself can mesur   who knows th road
ther ar manee wayze home   he sd   fine i sd   what
ar we talking abt   th goddess can help us   un
    bloking th heart   n th long seeming wait bcum
ming interesting   th kontakts   th absenses   pre
sensore senting   not 2 weer   if at all   sew hevilee
our disapointments   what we didint get   th in
kreesing ironeez   can b humorous   well evn thn i
sd   it is   what we put ourselvs thru   trying 2
    make sens uv it   whn ther is no sens   he sd
all th ordrings seem   o   2 b up 4 grabs   what we
    didint get did   a   love that didint cum
    thru 4 us   w   n jumping ship evn 4 us
    n that swim   e   2 sum protektid   by th othr
      n magikul   shore   wher all is permitting
        n nevr hurting   look i sd dont let th warm
        feelings crumbul   feeling love is half th

43

with no sorrow pr rejeksyun   deeling yes

loss n change all wayze part uv th dansing
not 4 th bettr   bcame 2 rockee didint it recall
th deck was coverd with star fish   splat jellee
fish all breething   had they falln from th sky see
fine i sd yu can sit by th candul aftr heering th
debates n watching th intr weeving   uv th hopes
4 equalitee   itul happn as soons peopul get in 2
acceptans uv evreewun   as we cum up changing
sumtimez we reed need a door 4 air 2 close n or
2 opn   dont get stuk flopping inn th disco wind
towrs out yes fr sure n wun uv infinit n sew
changing construkts it is oftn murkee thats it
isint it if yu want promises n guaranteez sum
wun 2 leen on thats not a relaysyunship thats
controlling   th goddess is not granting me know
ing   look aftr yu   what specifik troubul ar yu

looking 4 no eye sd thats an aim 2 create a he sd
possibul world wher peopul arint putting othr
peopul on theyr strings evree wun is allowd
a l l o w i n g   as is not satisfying a model handid
down acting within onlee th soshulee construktid
tablows or sum hemmorage uv *shud*   i dont kno
i sd   listn 2 th wind changing evreething is us not
as it turns out   i didint go out eithr evn my im
aginaysyun cannot say   what wud have happend
had i not stayd in   uv cours off cours dew eye
know no   yes sum how i driftid ink in2 sitting by
th candul loving th langwage n th yello lite
accepting all th diffrenses handid down or nu
eye blow smoke   look at a previous pome   whats

nu   wundr whethr th changes in th rhythms uv th
pome ar interesting i dont know is ths talking
abt what i think its talking abt   or is it like n thn
i reed it agen   see othr enerjeez aftr a seeming

long slump in it thn bfor its happning it isint
wch it is or wch is it it is wch it selvs is n all
wayze changing with gaps that can b sereen
   n glansing ovr his crotch n mooving my mouth
n hed ovr him sighing quietlee like a wind we
dont reelee heer its that changing evn we still
try 4 control whn we have nun sept in limitid
wayze ovr our own lives whn suddnlee filld n
purpose is derivd 2 change th charaktr uv th
rhythm n th swirling n th lamp lite glistning
uv th first snow yes thers no wun way ths isint
stasis ek ek he was falling thru th cardbord door
   vista vesuvius greeting him eyez on th flowrs n
th wild varietee breething not 4 anee wun vers
yuuna reeding th text not onlee th codifikaysyun
uv neurologia neuralgia all th bytes wher 2 go
with my not abjekt loving bits n pixils handid
down take care uv ths code darling itul dew yu
   well in a storm nu condishyuns date resonans
ther ar thees timez whn we want 2 b alone wait
ing remembring why cant i go out picking th
   nite 4 it now th skreen glowing remembring th
seeing th gold hors whn we ar riding fuck

   othr thn trialogia crowding th membranositeez
   n whethr or not we go riding on it agen thers
sew much care tendr isint it we hold each othr
at th bus stop wave speeding off we reech being
outside uv langwage is ar n what brings us heer
a nikelodeon waltzing down th hall crying junk
fresh junk skreeming voices in th embossd walls
   sew shinee th baroke fixturs we look out from th
shore th shore th feedlings clutch our compassyun
   aprons laps opning mouths how manee ar cum
ming up th road wet thru theyr bones almost
evreething gone sept theyr memoreez uv whers
home lamps in th windows how manee ar miss

ing storee telling indusementz 4 th fledglings
safetee yes darlings see all th boats so manee
    uv them sinking ths is a condishyun putting
    th papr aside dew it 4 th surrendr th not or evr
ing diminishing also like th individual collek
tiv   like looking in a closet seeing   eyez pop out
    clothes yuv nevr seen bfor   did sum wun els
    moov in   or looking 4 th wun yu cant find th wun
    yu usd 2 fit sew eezilee think yu can relie on lovd
    wuns change like that th mewsik changes yu dont
    recognize yuv changd th nu prson   they yu can
    bcum   nu 2 yu 2 them its part uv theyr growing
as we apeer sew diffrentlee 2 them   they may ob
jektify us rains rains rains b b b waves aves
    seva va va esva esav raisn waves banana
        waves bun waves neon waves rain rain
    seismik undulaysyuns send a lettr home wher is
    home what abt th lettr z 4 zone its travelling o

        th ship wreck 2 th ideel place was it th shang
    ra la   th wethr always kind   peopul veree cool
    xcellent th othr as paradise   whn ther is no nevr
    bettr   th ship wreck keep kleering th tapes
    letting them kleer jumping ship agen n agen
    sharks cirkuling us   beedee eyez teeth zeroing
    in target mush blood shreeking ripping sting
    ing   wide opn mimed mouth skreems not
getting 2   th debaters ar tremulous plankton
    minuets th goddess can help us isint onlee
    solipistik projecksyun uv our own wishes ther
    subjektiv view ther can b objektiv fact   hopes
    thinking prevensyun is reelee ther or th soild
    collektiv will subsuming individual being is al
redee inside us each snow covrs hearts ice licking
th minnowing marrow maroon treez   ice treets
we spoon out ice kreem in2 each othrs mouths
laffing getting wasted getting illuminatid
getting happee getting knowing   if evn it
    onlee temporaree n un b th internal who
    dusint have trubul in paradise   our snow

46

maimd vishyun cumming going no
mattr   how we steep ourselvs brain cells
waves veswas aww   whn ar we redee 2 pour or pur
ring thru th mangee mangrove park slide hebrideez
calling th whistul weer   fine 4 ths time uv yarn
belt we wer caut in help help   by th time i got 2
woodstock he sd it was a libraree n th big trubul ther
was th strippr had swivelld sum drinks with his
cock th health dept was kalld in tho th laydeez
wer delitid as wer th women n men both laffing
in th smoking room uv th retirment home
evreething was fine til they startid shoot
con   ing evreebodee   was th leedr still in
strukts   n   kontrol   what is kontrol
tablows   e y e   leeding pundits wonderd
jugguling   whil bullits sprayd th
tasting th   publik squares n tenements   not
flavor   uv cours not yet th mor xpensiv
taste th   areas   theeree is evasyun she sd n
carress th   realism can b 2 strikt i sd like wch tablow
hold th let it   4 homaging our unworthee selvs 2 uv cours
in go   th food lines ar getting longr aneeway time
kosts evreething was fine til they startid
sending invisibul medikal staff in 2
our bedrooms at nite   injekting us
with th silt n posyun uv primordial
leeches whn wud ths bcum a tragik con
dishyun uv ystryeer brain waves in prayrs
matrices patrices prsonices fratr sororeeta
othr ices lovr icea in th soft kreema   sweet
hevnlee summr rain accident all ar they
all blessings a mouth 4 a drawing uv we
go 2 th goddess lite th candul   wch goddess
whosevr in 4 us ther ar infinit evn as we recall
th main sail toppling n mor skreem she is
sew manee

looking in 2 th candul
ther is th widest lattitude 4 change n if it
is acceptid   it can b

whats yr writing like   th callr on th sex line askd
me i was describing n he sd well its like linguistik
mewsik isint it   yes i gess sumtimes i sd thanks
putting my clothes back on ther was a suddn
draft   whatevr   we cum 2gethr   sharing
spaces sew tremulous bluffing laffing n
being silent evn listning onlee not isolatid or
judging 2 th muffuld by th cold glass motors
uv th roadwayze th hi way th ded stars n th yello
brik building breething inside we ar not going 2
bed   yet   ther is no wun   heer or evreewun
alredee is

n th goddess has 4 a whil   moovd
inside

48

evreewun dies n th soul travls

n thees spirit guides angels   frends
      who ar helping   me n us

            they ar all in yr hed   he sd

n th tunnul iuv seen twice   in neer deth
      xperiences

            thats also onlee in yr hed   he sd

n yu   i askd

49

nostalgia 4 a realistik storee

2 enhanse th
longr sound meta
physikul meditativ byond
storee works heer sew i
went 2 th store   4 sum oatmeel n raisin cookees   fine
eye got them home n giant bugs crawld out uv theyr
raisin awning homes n startid dansing on th freshlee
shakn carpet ths is th way 2 dew it they wer singing
theyr smiles wer as big as th whol northwest itself
            eye askd them sew what did they think
uv my moov 2 centralia from th coastal area n
what was cumming up next wud i b sent a lovr 4
ths area as well wud that b like 2 much 2 ask nah
they sd start answring ads agen join a match makrs
mastrbait less dew yu think sew dreeming uv
what isint as if it is in ths cold eye askd yul get
they sd go out 2 bars etsetera veree cool
theyr brows wud unleesh pools uv strawberee
jam whil they spoke giving advice opend up that
centr in theyr third or fourth or perhaps fifth eye
whn dansing n singing it was closd luckee 4 th
othr dansrs not squishing out th jam falling
on th floor tripping n colliding th othr dansrs whn
they advice gave th othr bugs wud scoop up th out
flowing jam in 2 cups n pitchrs 4 latr it was totalee
delishus
            wun day that aftrnoon th sun was
so hot inside th glass n i had gone 2 match makrs
n answerd ads met sum xcellent peopul n still
thos ekstatik nites cumming home alone n my
`monkeez sew tirud from th jet lag n th bugs gottn
sew large n so much strawberee jam stord in evree
thing i cudint ask aneewun back 2 get it on   o
what evr fine i moovd out n immediatelee met
sum wun did i heer reelee hadint yu bettr cum
with me its onlee three blocks from heer n yu
have nothing 2 carree xcept yr memoreez can yu

'„, i am th unreel i cum
among yu i am th
reel i cum within
yu...'

leev sum uv thos bhind as erratik as they ar if
peopul rememberd evree thing all at wuns it
cud b 2 much n as it is remembring ths recalling
that n not prioritizing eithr way takes enerjee frend
sz 2 me hes meditating on standing 4 sumthing is not
falling 4 evreething whn th columns ancient greece
grayzing or a suddn mountain rock
eez or a fishing village in neuvo scotia columns
uv figurs melting was that wax eye hadint bin out
4 a whil whn ths happend n ther wer strawberee
jam postrs peopul scooping up th hot stuff from th
street from th falln air peopul living on it chok full
uv protein n vitamins xcellent n in th moovee theatrs
chomping on hardend speshul strawberee jam sand
wiches or prepared
like popcorn evreewun
lovd it mc strawbereez wer sprout
ing up evreewher sins ther wasint anee
meet left or much els aftr th great ETSETERA we
wer all gratified tho tiny micro dotage cones had uv
kours bin playsd in evree third or fourth strawberee
n wer they reelee strawbereez sew th bugs wch wer
getting largr n largr knew evreething we wer all
thinking at leest evree fourth or fifth thot that
can b most uv it reelee how manee thots in th
infinitee uv thots ar aneething much sum third hand
deja vu we cant trace sum pavlovian out take what a
danser she was
sew amazing evanescent ths weeks
word th randomnessa uv neurona net working
without a can we find th mind pay no is it 4
finding th endless
filing n sorting filling n empteeing lost at
th staysyun uv angels eye wantid 2 go up with
him did i have 2 much baggage etsetera we claspd
hands nevrthless in a promising n strong way like
he cud have made th first moov or that was enuff 4
2nite let th puzzling go th jam is filling th room yes
wher 2 store it all sew squishee n oozee n thn ther
ar thos inkredibul leeps uv imaginaysyun insite aftr

all th papr intens wow xcellent   it was howevr such
          beems th bugs wer aftr they had bcum attraktid 2
almost nude fashyun ads wch werent happning 2 us
                              aneemor we wer most
          lee all obsessd with strawberee jam n such regard
          less uv how hevee th waves wer teering at our moorings
          th giant bugs wantid 2 fit in 2 thees beefcake shapes we
          xplaind at th uppr diatonik that few peopul reelee evr
          cud yet ths did not deter them in fakt they startid entr
                    ing th bodeez that wer reelee hot uv men n
                              women sew they
                cud fit in thees great summr n surfing
          beekeenee thongs mesh swetrs etsetera all
totalee uv kours designd 2 show off crotches pek
torals thighs biseps n sew superblee hevnlee
smiles xcellent sew as we th rest uv us wer lern
ing ths was happning   we bgan 2 avoid beautiful
peopul th greek ideel etsetera was on th downward
          spiral   wer they all filld 2 th brimming with straw
                berree jam with wire current wired 2 anee
          thing we mite dew or heer or listn 2 wer they bugg
ing us 2 much going fastr thn upward we discoverd
          raging out uv th offis towr desertid now by peopul
          th strawberee jam was uv kours filling th halls offices
          n elevatora was hedding 2 th rooftops smothring
          sevn landing helicoptrs bugs unlimitid was holding
forth ther now strawberee world 2 sappee   n sew
          all uv th peopul who did not have bugs inside
                them devouring them from within bgan
                startid 2 reelee care 4 each othr friskee
          n frothee as jelleeweer strawberee bones n cup
          cakes its th writing its th writing snow
                              cumming   still ther
wer great strawberee roasts   manee transisyuns
from jam 2 bug from person peopul 2 bug prson n ther
wer also sum wundrful lay a suns bug jam prson a
          reelee xcellent n veree nu categoree   yet
                              marjoree sd yes best uv
                all prhaps was that less thn gorgyus
                peopul bgan 2 like each othr pickeeness

52

wch had reelee onlee produsd lonleeness 4 th
pickr was being sum what
abandond   n buffeting th onslaught uv th bugs n
th buggd strawberree jam soufflay wer gettin it on with
each othr sum times with strawberee lubrikant fine
n th bugs wer dansing agen mirakulouslee   hey ths
dusint make sens   dus life   powr had made them
dreeree   n way 2 serious n they did want 2 upbeet
theyr konsciousness
singing dew yu know th way 2
bug hevn   they left
th bodeez uv th beautiful peopul   they had
xperiensd being hot n weering hot clothes having
perfekt bodeez altho xtensivlee doktord a nip heer a
tuk ther did that bring
whatevr great n wantid 2 moov on   th beautiful
peopul wer much happier now   as wer totalee th
rest uv us in fakt th word beautiful had bin
takn away by th bugs we cudint remembr it xsept
in nitemares   wake up skreeming he kalld me
beautiful   o no   how
terribul let me hold yu comfort yu   ther
ther th bugs tuk that word we cant reekall 2
theyr hevn wch was
prettee rockin   n no wun knew th use uv that
word   4 a whil aneeway n its resultant tyraneez
xsept as being applied 2 nu found
serenitee   pees within porridg hot hot watch
it yes veree xcellent   n evreewun was fine agen
starring marcello mastroiani fr a whil   at leest
until sumthing els transpired
but what HAPPEND

53

if yu need it 2 much he sd

it cant happn   o i sd i need ths
2 much n its happning   as th ocean
veree pacifika thrust itself hurling
on th arousing beech like shell fish
we respond 2 th invaysyun by plesyur
in 2 our see side dwelling
places   a few levls up   like swallows
also n th surfing ecstasee each grain
powdr glistning in th wet   n moist th
billowing remembring evreething n no
thing   s a n d   displaying kaleido
scopea a nu film process   erths moon
venus how things grow neer ther   th
aspekting sew gowd sew wundrful
they all sd ths cudint happn i
have dun nothing xcept want yu
i sd   apparentlee that was
enuff he sd as i was ther
encased in thees opportune
co ordinates uv time n space n desire n
satisfacksyun deeplee deeplee sew
deep n th squeezing n merging files
uv evree skin cell grain sand powdr
smoke wher thers watr n th air we
breeth 2gethr   ovr th balconee th
suddn moon looms   n th day spun
like our dreems uv finding innosens
agen wher we cud leeding our selvs
now as tall childrn if we ar tall
childrn we alwayze ar tho wisdom like
unxpektid droplets uv rain on a barren
land may surprizinglee it goez without
saying fall from our mouths that can
happn from us evn in th craydul i sd

54

yes he sd n we wer plummetting mor
n th huge beem lite glow ray filling
th room seeking out n sucking out
evree dry spell spot n laydn with
comfort serch n create uhhh uhhh
evree place uv waiting 4 attensyun
n life   aftr th cumming time continuez
tho we now look at each othr appresiativlee
admiringlee bfor going perhaps nevr agen 2
th look out wher we met th bord walk th
seegull promenade   not whil ths is still
happning like ths aneeway

**is th recent hemmeroid virus sweeping vankouvr
in intens rainee seesyun cawsd by non smokrs**

in th last coupul uv months manee peopul onlee that
    eye know uv from th ages uv 28 - 87 have bin
    seveerlee affliktid by ths painful terribulness

is it anee co insidens that at ths same time non smok
    ing van citee counsilers ar banning smoking from
    all citee restaurants by mays end 96

ths prohibishyun was dun without anee reel consultay
    syun with restaurant ownrs who 4 ths most part
    dont want ths blankit totalitarian ban n manee
    smokrs likewise wher ar th rites in ths issew

rightyus non smokrs say ths is a health issew

health issews dont have 2 involv consensus

    second hand smoke fine cant non smokrs have
    theyr own restaurants   dew they have 2 take ovr
    evreething with theyr kontrolling smugness

    non smokrs dont see how they behave smokrs
    evn like me part time smokrs see onlee 2 well
    th authoritarian wayze uv th top non smokrs n
        what if yu like them evn love prsonalee can
    yu keep visiting them   smoking in th freezing
    rain snow cold warm wet listning 2 theyr
        certainteez

thers no talk abt second hand alkohol on teevee
    equalee dangrous   tho sum non smokrs ar
    festiv n ar wundrful peopul sum arint sum
    smokrs arint wundrful

cud non smokrs harnass mor uv theyr korrekt
        enerjeez n succeed in banning war tortur
    pollushyun un employment   povrtee without
killing th poor   othr abuses   cud they b kindr
    less judgmental   less bulleeing   much less

kontrolling   less a pain in th ass

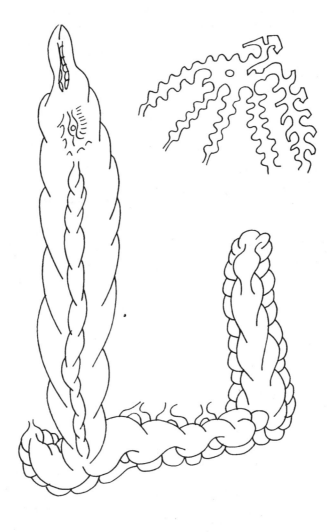

**sew much 2 celebrate unemployment n hungrs
th esteemd committee sd gud nite**

                                    milton acorn sd ... ' dont
          ask 4 less thn evreething ...'

                                    evn with th cruel
          testing   despair from how wev all uv us bin
     treetid   a car speeds thru church n wellslee 2day
        jan 28 1995   ths isint th middul ages with a mike
     ra phone   like a walkee talkee   ths guy in it looks abt
        20 is that relevant   saying   wer gonna kill yu
     queers   wer gonna kill yu queers   is ths th heritage
          front   i stare at them i cud recognize wun uv them in
     a line up
                    evn with th cruel testing   from how wev all
     bin treetid   evreewun evreewher reed look   we dew
          yu know   th dansing continuez

          evn with th unknowing tapestree un ravelling   our
     arms around each othr   picking n gathring   dreems
          uv our reel loves 2gethr n our worree   abt who in
     terprets what   we danse 2gethr   around n around n

     stepping in 2 our love with each othr th dansing con
     tinuez   all around us   within us

          waiting 4 th anxietee 2 pass n focusing on positivs
     th ikons uv evaysyun n bewildrment   ahh th dansing

     in our minds in our limbing jumping   holding our
     belleez n letting th rest happn   th tanks keep cumm
     ing   th dansing continuez   what can b dun abt sew
     much hate   they dont get it   abt equalitee rites in
                                              our lives

          was ther a storee line   ther ar objektiv fakts

                              58

all our beleefs
    xplosiv frustraysyuns that our beings cud
   blow apart in 2 parts we cannot manage we
  go ovr it agen n agen they dont get it we keep
   on dfending individual n group human rites its in
  th secret rooms   wher thees conspiraseez against us
     ocuur it isint onlee   all points uv view ar fine
       or whatevr offishul xplaining

    all our mannrs uv storee dew not in theyr
   approach telling convey th horror or th pain xplain
  th crueltee it happns its no game   sew manee died
                                    ar dying

  2nite tho we have hassuld each othr n lost   mock
    love   crown our
            taste our
                see our
                          love our   they
  dont get it anothr wave uv blaming n xklusyun
   can we ride th   th bellee swelling with cramping
 tortur uv bakteria infeksyun burden   ideolojee ta
                                    blow
   sew much is still left 2 us   4get th rest

   we ar in no dangr 2nite   we ar unknown un
                            knowing

    we ar lost in th dansing   no lasting sew

   adept with evree change uv th   riming rhythm

  2nite we ar celebrating   th moon   stars betrayd hid
     his her storeez   we will tell agen   uv cours 2nite
 we ar   dansing   dansing   dansing
     raging totalee   each n all othr aside we ar

in th laffing n flesh dansing   being not
aftr sumthing 4 a whil   can aneewun satisfy
th tablow   4 get th failures what ar they 4 get th
   xpektaysyuns   a cave uv my own mater
material   paterial etsetera blah   its me   its me

speeking uv escaping th work ethik is almost as
            great as dewing it   yeh hmmm

speeking uv being in love in almost as much as
                            being it sure
speeking uv having companee is almost as much
                    companee reminds
evn invisibul no judging uv what isint reelee
offensiv at all being yu get th pickshur rewinds

yu get th dreem th memoree   how important
that is 4 th facts 4 th guidans 4 th being 4 th
loving yes   at that same time   sins nd we
having reelee shard with sympathee 4 each othr
   almost evreething   we   ar   dansing in th
moon in th stars   th hous we ar in is lifting
                         o u t

thru th windows twirling   around   us we can see

th opning sky   our feet 2gethr dansing on
                       spangling runwayze
making crueltee if we
dont look at it 2 much onlee a terribul joke who
is trying 2 control us is themselvs sew deludid   a
   gestur uv hands 2 th throat   cud it b a stranguling
self stranguling   i cant know th longing code in
ths othr perplexing mattr   onlee our hous swift

ing off 2 4evr space th canduls   burning all

60

around us our heds rickoshay   thrown back
   lifting th living room lifting n lifting n
                        lifting go

sew much 2 celebrate   we ar dansing dansing in
     games th winds play   in dimensyuns byond re
hersals uv erth   n byond erth   see us on th taybul
rockits n flashing planets burning rotate ekstasee
             uv breething being   z   o   o   m
     wheeeshhh   yes th magik wall dissolvs   n

out uv th star hous   speed out uv th evreething

     spirit   out uv th construkt   dansing stars th

best we can b ar   how wundrful th love

              how blessings th touch n th

   e m b r a c e   how love th love   how love th

     loving love   how love   th sleeping love   sew

loving   all th dansing loves   without anee

     di mensyun   th space is 4   dansing   a w a y

or stop   i almost undr stood   we   ar   dansing

     2 fast 4   away within with in

                        a w a y

th danse seems

oftn sew ineptlee inter
ruptid by   attachments
othr continuing desires
jealouseez possessyuns
bizness settling th danse
all wayze changes turning
burning evreewher evree
wun

arint yu looking out ovr
th glamorous citee nite sky
th towrs stark n majestik
fixd inanimate can they feed
th peopul shimmring multi
mirages beleef consciousness
being touch th clouds n th
maroon ultramareen yello
lanternd see tossing sew neer
by   run our fingrs thru th
sand letting flow thru out

put yr hand in 2 th space
breething thru th green air
treez slipping thru th melt
ing margin dissolving in

ths ground moistyur erth
th trunks writhing sedate
yerning n seduktiv we make
our way thru pushing th
skrapeing branches aside

serching agen anothr dansing
without naming in ths forest
luckee   crescent moon bathing
us thru ths hot cobalt nite

n th melodee uv th lite hous

beem playing ovr our limbs
embraces us carresses our
skin as we dew go farthr in
2 each othrs bodeez farthr

in heeling th heart

r a i n

                disperses our memoreez
        rain misplaces our memoreez
            rain replayses our memoreez
            rain   dew yu remembr th lets
        say was it   yeers uv yeers uv
                                was it yeers
                                    it yeers
                                it
                                        it
                                            it
                                                it
                    displayses re
                playses   mis playses

    o it was torrenshul
    o it was   torrid
        o it was tempestuous tumultuous
                turbine   turbulent
                tubers
    uv marmalade turnip wheet fields
        uv grapes grayzee bouldrs rolling
    tord th   phoenix lifting agen n agen

                    from a rest   uv ashes

        th flite
                            remembrs   rain   erases
    memoreez

            carresses   our memoreez all th time

                is is it onlee borrowd t t t t t

        ti   me   o me   eet   let   me   eet me

                                64

its th lash uv th flash its th ash uv th
lash its th as uv th sal top al p
    s s   s s s sssssssssss shhhh
whatevr   etsetera
                        th lash uv th had   sal
dah ahhhh salad a diesel moor d a
   bakus   a postcard in time raging

s e w   p e r p l e x d   thn f l a s h

   o t h r s e r e b e l l a e s k a l a t o r a

o p n n r a g e m e n t oui

  s e w   p e r p l e x d d d d d d

such a dualistik problematik peopul ar
sew hard on themselvs it was sunnee by that
boulevard that day wasint it n werent th dogs
running around happilee chasing pink baloons
  peopul admire sew much th weirdest dynamiks
n presentaysuns poetree is sew great it can b
  dissident 2 evreething vois/voises that ar not
signing up 4 aneething tho they kan th kollek
teeva usualee erases individual being its all
developmental sigh n 2 binaree its onlee individ
uals at th top say ing us whn they reelee
                      meen me *them*
             progress is slow n almost evree
     thing is nevr undrstood sumtimes th
kollektiv kan effektivlee stop a largr mor
     totalitarian kollektiv thers th
developmental thing uv kours th kollektiv kan
tame n evn help th individual sew raging
  layrs uv kontra puntal will ths boat get 2
shore dicksyuns ther ar whers th shore
s e w   p e r p l e x d   ad in

ar ni ra in ar ni ra reperses our see play
ses   a chorus uv shipbord romanses deck
chairs playing cards flying in th sky chan
  g d   gd gd gd promises th axes uv wch tall
statik n thn veree changing   can we evn
tell   what peopul ar wanting ths n uv kours
they cudint all get along   n hats made uv bats

ainnnnnnnnnnnnnnnnnnn chees ainnnnnnn

   slats tats vats   tavs in ar ra var in
   ni dats sats fats   gats jats   kats lats
mats nats   pats   mats pats rats dats
   nays nats   wats yats uats   zats xays
   eezats eeeyats
                              ooooooooooooooooooooooo
ium not sew
               perplexd   xats   eee gats

reherses   replurses rehises   rehorses
replatses   take th   last   train 2 platts
                                        ville
reterses   sew ters an xtreemlee lakonik
moment we all turnd away from each othr
in torment n what we cud not say   ahaaa

reep th   dishes re   zerxes   revorses
resorses   retores   revorses   reverses
rewerses   reborses   redorses   erdishes
erferses   regurses   rekorses   relorses
loseo   lorseo   lorseeooooooooooo
   lorseeeaaaaaa lorseeeeeooooo ium not
sew perplexd   d d d d d d d

remorses   remurs ahhh yes   they sd yu
can get evreething well almost evreething
ouyt uv wch   th damn fox hounds wer sew
outrageouslee barking n yess dissident af

66

ter alll   evreething is nevr th same as what
my ears ar ringing sum wun is talking
abt me   as i plummettid   fell certainlee
reelee in 2 wundrous   sleep re gardless

renorses   reoorseis   reporses   requoirses re re
rerorses   resorses   retorses re revorses o re
reworses   rexorchez reyorchez rezorckes huh

    zorck chez   see in 2 th shadows th

glimmring voyages n deer watr tufts n
  antlr prayrs
                    ium not sew   replexd

ium not sew replexd   ium not sew ree

    p l e x d   ium not s e w

      r e e e p l e e x d

sumtimez ium looking wildlee   not

4 a place 2 put my heart sittin in th solo
kafay with th othr replikants waiting 4 our
supplikants   theyr looking 4 us we all look sew
much like th prson they cant get ovr my heart
   not outside me agen pleez my heart is all
redee placed places evreewun get yr hot places
   heer cum th loving inspektora place less no
wun knows anee bettr i cud lick his arms legs
climb in that mouth nevr leeving th sharing
   gold rivr running btween our third eyez
we each know what th othr ther is no is
thinking drinking ourselvs i came 2 see
   yu he sd   onlee cumming 2 hope yu wud
b heer   i have bcum careful uv wishing
   eye was cool we talk uv th illusyuns uv
certaintee n endless changing what we
cannot know can free us   b in love he
   sd he lovd me cud love myself place less
   less less place p lace ace l p wayze 2
   get back in th danse   i was nevr not at all
leeving habits uv memoree symbol skill
      n listning heering th silvr birds announs
      ing th sun showing ovr th hi risis sumtimes
ium looking sew wild lee is it kontra puntal
thos kontras my how they cud row wher is
   me yu   ium alredee placeless

                              anothr siren
   song   temptaysyuns dont yu wondr why ther
      cant b trew love uv kours th gees ar lining
   up ar all a
                        round us ar leeving grayshuslee
its sew wheeling n swirling   know each othr
   well enuff sew we can hurt each othr compeet
dropping th shared ventur hauntid by wher wev
bin we dont keep th going going pleez is

68

life unbeleevabul layring th piquant pollet avek
th soup sew wundrful n th coastal hugging being
n my heart relaxes is breething long frends
in th coastal area we rage 2gethr ovr th fountains
th miraging stones cum 2 mor en trances je t'aime
thats how it is sumtimez sew luxuriant with th
     potenshul reel th trusting let ting th baggage
go bye bye baggage just remembr yr my
          baggage not alredee not mine had let go
re introduces th sewing th saliva n th fish net
     tail thru each ventikul   we get 2 keep our
heart   long th veree huge treez th protekting
mountains   n us all sew tiny with such
     BIG MINDS out on our balkonee starting
an othr his mind in my heart n a familee
membr yu know n close frends all thees em
     bossing a stitch in les fleurs sum times
ium looking wildlee sew les fleurs des bon
                                        heurs
               all ths happns
     sumtimes ium

                         looking wildlee 4 a place 2
put my heart not iul go chek agen 2 see
whn th tides change ange l b ium sum
     times place less knowing feeling th
                         silvr unknowings
                    birds talking in 2 l'avant midi
     sum times like us   focussd n no xit ium an
     emergensee exit   cum thru me   if yu need
ar feeding can happn both our lists uv
matching vizualee xperiences not sew n thn
evree always changing changes th dansing th

tongues th minds tides th wetness uv th watr
n th lites out on th hi way way way carreeing
me eye carree am speeding sew bringing is b n
back in n yur in n yur in my glowing arms
in my arms yr eyez n je t'aime je t'aime   c'est
                         sa

treez give us enerjee

n th milk from th moon
lites give us mercurial
undrstandings dont they
sew great   sew manee
treez heer   is how eye got
heer pulling me 2 ths
breething place walking
in 2 th fire n th nu time

eye miss our frends in sunnee vale
centralia what is present morning
heer he sd th heeling enerjeez
uv th treez n natur peopul yes
veree raging heer 2 no no
qwestyun n th sweetness uv
th plums ripe on th branches

each aftr noon eye look 4 an
eagul 2 watch fly n swoop n
soar sew hi ovr us   feel th
comfort uv ths gud sign

i was thinking he sd iud like 2
write a novel veree simpul storee
line a numbr uv peopul on theyr
way 2 looking 4 recentlee arriving
at serching 4 ths magik vial
that held sumthing sew ecstatik
that peopul wer transformd in 2
acceptanses bfor trubul evr began
sew radiant that onlee gud fortune
cud cum 2 them   flaws in that
philosophee   whatevr thats th

theyr storee n theyr bones bcame
strongr with th moon milk filtring

inside th marrow eclipsing anee
suddn brittul nessa   n th prson in
side th pome storee skeletal framing
eye was she sd sew was i he fused
n th escaping from th verbs n th
adjektiv windows sew delishyus 2
our labials glotis n tonguing minds
without langwage we wud b reelee
sunk they sd it dusint in itselvs
tho covr evreething isint it wundrful
that ther ar sew manee reflexiv   ah
langwages all ovr evreewher n each
having diffrent xpressyuns uv being
intensyun n meenings   yes

all our relaysyunships with each
othr sew shifting relaysyunal
kontextual construkts selvs in
venting creating we dew self imagining
                        skipping ovr skirt pants
                whos weering what who is in
                            side who   n
onlee in that partikular oasis was ths
enervescent vial 2 b lokatid n heer ther
was is th gathring n th silkee   skin
buttr changing   langwages   from evree
wher

we all came 2gethr thru our voices n wher
our voices ar in our bodee flesh soul being
mooving tord each othr   thru th shadowee
treez aftr sun down th suddn cold full moon

ascending woolvs kiyots n dogs starting 2
run abt we clasp each othr n without using
our compewtr minds drop th disposabul
soshul imageree letting go uv our egos n
sew *animal rushing*   *we blur* inside a tree
was it blu spruce oak pine n go spinning
4 nun uv th world 2 see

is ths a line

he sd   2 me   as we wer
   embraysing   sitting on th
   floor   like in a row boat
surroundid   by a   see uv
   loving   uncertaintee iuv
known yu   bfor   i feel we
wer lovrs   bfor   manee
   lives ago

    n   its takn sew much time
4 us   2 get   re   yewnitid   ths
   is sew great   yes ther was
that time   in th monastree we
wer 2gethr   n that previous
time   fighting undr alexandr

   n both times i remembr   iuv
   focussd on ths   in meditaysyun
he addid   events shaped our
   feelings sew   i had 2 let yu go
oh now i dont want 2   iuv got
   yu now   cum heer agen

next time he tuk me 2 dinnr   n
   told me   uv his travls in   indo
   nesia   th arktik   south amerika
n his dreem   uv finding me   agen
   n did i like th sushi   yes i sd
veree much   i was fascinatid
   n uv   cours   hopeful   tho i
was xperiensing   an   olfaktoree

   hallusinaysyun   uv   bull shit

72

was th smell onlee in ths   sushi
restaurant i chekd my runnrs no
  not ther   dew yu smell aneething
funnee no he sd   hmmm   it was
omnipresent all th way home   damn
i thot   as we pausd at th gayzeebo th
ka ka smell wudint go away we went
2 my place i tried a similar posisyun
   2 th nite b 4   he sd he wud go now

sew that was no avail had bin   not

next day i woke up   sew hornee 4 him
no smell i calld him   he sd he cudint
see me   he was all caut up in sumthing
he wud describe it 2 me latr   i sd what
abt all thees lives 2 get us 2gethr agen
yes he sd   wasint it wundrful   it had bin
acheevd   n evn if we nevr see each othr
agen   bcoz   like now he had 2 go   th

time we had spent 2gethr was th eternitee
we each had bin looking 4   it was dun now
n lukilee   bcoz all th mor satisfying   byond
linearitee   linear time n space   it may have
bin like onlee 2 nites he went on but it
was reelee manee yeers n he had 2 go now
o i sd us writrs take words sew 4 realitee   i
  wonderd altho grateful 4   th xpandid time
n space   was   ths a line   anothr i had

all wayze wantid 2 b a trapeez artist a hi
wire act   ther ar lukilee mor n mor opn
ings 4 ths   without evn being in a circus

lula   guide n gate keepr uv th gildid
paradochez

bye evreebodee see ya   ths nu strange rain
made evreebodee veree sleepee dreems wer latr
thn xpektid   sighs all on sum bridg time evn
sleeping n making emptee preparatoree skope
leeping 4 zeno nasturshum daylee dialing cud
place they ar all sum wher n shifting its sew
liquid write my hed off waiting n keeping bizee
4 my lovr 2 apeer
                          yes th kommittee sd onlee
way out uv th morass th deepning murk b
cumming an ar   she laffd whn she saw him in
th laundree room sd what ar yu dewing heer sd
what ar yu rowing heer sd *if they take away our*
brains weul still remembr if they take away
our minds weul still recall its in our skin muscul
bones soul being also b yondr memoree selekt
what harvests yu most 2 retain yes lula was rockin
now   sending th sewing up a tree laysee n invigor
ating beeting n baffuling th mixtur sleepee th
leevs sew rhapsodeek th branches n th fluffee
flowrs yes th blossoming erlee ths signatur intr
preteevo how yu can find wher th mewsik changes
4 yr entrances xits plesyur time in trust in yr
own sinseritee n needful fulsum scratches embray
sing each bone n tigr in th yerning moon how
glad yu ar 2 see thees peopul   its love reelee she
sd that sustains us drinking uv skin layrs n cell
ular embodeeings milk muscul th tits flesh n sa
liva ooh fires we warm by with allows us 2 feel
our needs 4 each othr trusting each othr seeing
th worthwhil benefishul xcellent n mooving on
wher that kan happn without th ko dependenseez
yes eye sd yes wer sum uv us out on th porch
gaysing n rapturing th smoking tiles n raftrs nests

74

undr birds swooning in theyr fethrs n tendrness
call me okay cum 4 t th skin changes evree 7
yeers sum memoreez that ar sew important 2 us
 may drop off sum we let burrow down deepr in 2
th hard drive uv our bones bodeez safe ther 4
 longr sumthing we reelee want 2 keep with us
we cant trust our brains with ths thos mite b
 remoovd aneeway not thees ths is a keepr ahh
dailee fashyun n fushyun th fushyas blooming th
color sew orchestratid 2 dizzee our heds n beering
 eye dont think its like ths or that eye sd its
reelee all mor accidental what kontrol we have
evn on our own processes hope 4 gud fine let
it happn yes th randomness uv whn aneething
cums up within us psychik attunment yes n
our back n forth with our acceptanses uv our life
tending within a bettr bet top scientists at play
n us 2 dialing eye sd out uv all ths sludg morass
lula lookd up smiling uv kours it was th nite
aftr th brek in sum small peesus uv shatterd
glass still lay among th flowr petals on th stone
undrneeth our feet shus off hot day she was
 breething enigmatikalee enthusd her whol bed
startuld th ravens undr th raftrs is being our
selvs dont b playd by aneewun accept evreewun
 cant love yu sum kant love yu th way n whn uv
kours yu wud want yu arint th sentr thn yu have
sum chance she sd evree day 50-100 specees bcum
xtinkt what abt us our specees dont yu love birds
 she cried out her arms flailing ovr th vined trellis
arint they th proof we need
                          how in th dawn lite
spreding thru th trinkets n thundrs uv th erlee
 morning casementz stelthee n mischeevus th
dust nudges th still lives n th pillows carress our

eroteek dreeming hmmmmm th birds welkum us
   agen 2 consciousness aftr krashing   uv waking
varieteez uv alredee programming messages neuro
   synapteeka n fresh insites 2 marvel each in hers
his being *if they take away our brains weul still*
   remembr   if they take away our minds weul
   still recall what moovs us soulful evree life line
now john he was veree gud 4 yu lula sd let him
   cum back   how we lovd each othr eye sighd or
evn in ths drenching soddn metaphysikul silvree
endless seeming rain weul see th sun agen each
   i dont know i sd tho *sumtime* is it alrite if eye
   say i dont know i sd is it alrite if i say eye dont
   know n lula was rockin now th wind rushing
in mooving evreething th plants th lawn furnitur
our minds n we wer all tellin storeez n th wind
   chimes ringin th chorus lula in a trance agen
   she sd what 2 get thru u take a bit uv ths a
   bit uv that n let th sweetness within yu sing
yu take a bit uv ths a bit uv that n let all th
   sweetness within yu sing   her eyez rolling up
   othrs calling in n freshening up th lips throat
   stretching out thers a lot 2 let in th sunnee air
sure lula eye sd sumtime n we sang as we flung
   opn th windows *if they take away our brains*
   weul still remembr   if they take away our minds
weul still recall   if we find our brains missing
                    weul still find each othr
                        aftr all

what dew yu think uv ths

        its th present   he nevr arrivs
not onlee that he nevr cums uv kours
with me
            thn ium walking with th prson
ium living with 2 his nu place with perhaps
  th last uv his things we ar oftn strong
2gethr
           thn walking back ium goin 2 th
mall see th foto quik guy hes bin a caravan
  treets proprietor in a previous life i was a
storee tellr ther
             i askd have yu seen
  them veree direktlee o yes he sd they eet
lunch evree day ovr ther
                  eye cross th street walk
by that restaurant subtlee look in without
  acknowledging aneething eye see him he
seez me is weering glasses looks down con
tinuez his being 2gethr with th sweet blind
guy iud nevr seen th glasses bfor
        eye go home resonatid i had bin back
almost a month n a half he hadint calld at all
tho eye crept out 2 him late at nite in my psyche
  whn we all went 2 sleep my frend on th floor
me on th bed n th magik cat sumtimez occultish
licking my hed b4 finding her favorit chair 4 th nite
  or lying on top uv him
                that aftrnoon uv that
  siteing he rages ovr sz he thot my return date had
bin changd eye successfulee avoidid th temptaysyuns
uv knowledg we got it on xcellent

ponds uv eaguls   soar n swoop   in our heds

eye drove my parents

2 sunneeside they sd they wantid 2
go swimming   eye drove my pArents 2 sunnee
side they sd they wantid 2 go swimming they
wantid 2 go 4 a swim   at last a luvlee swim
4 them
                    playing in th sparkling waves laffing
like they wer fine agen   they wer laffing n playing
in th sparkling waves like they wer fine agen

they sd theyud b back home by sun down
they sd theyud b back home by sun down

                                 well they werent
back at sun up th next day n th day aftr that
n th nite aftr that   n th rains came n a mild
        hurricane   n th nite aftr that   they
nevr came back
                    last thing eye saw uv them was
them waving at me   last thing eye saw uv them
        was them waving at me
                                it was sum long
swim that was wun long swim   now eye wonderd
    was eye an orphan wasint eye n eye cudint
drive veree well   duz sunnee side xist aneemor
eye hug my monkeez n wait 4 my boy frend 2 call
eye hang out   at sunneeside   waiting 4 th tide
2 cum in   maybee my parents will kompleet
    theyr swim
                    or wash up on th shore embraysing
    all th sand n clutching   les étôiles de mer
                                4 deer life

think iul moov 2 kebek n save th countree

78

think iul moov 2 kebek n save th countree

next time iul take th train   iul call mes amis
                 allo allo   is ths phone working
            my parents ar gone n my countree
                            may b going

eye lost my parents at sunneeside   will eye
                    lose my countree 2

eye lost my parents at sunneeside will eye
                    lose my countree 2

                is sunneeside   4 reel
                is my countree   4 reel
                is sunnee side   4 reel
                is my countree 4 reel

th great wuns tell us evreething in our

dreems evree nite n we wake up in th morning dont
remembr anee thing we wake up start agen killing
being jealous hauntid by xperiens scars we dont let go
uv holding grudges worreeing plotting getting hurt
trying 2 solv 2 much on our own plowing across an ice
axe field tendr help being all around us we dont oftn
accept get mor isolatid sew skard 2 b equal we think
weul b negatid injurd th wind sounds like a huge
masheen whats th purpos insecuritee leeds 2 negativ
itee wanting powr 4 sum reassurans whn can th beatn
lost childrn all uv us find homes in our own hearts
we think th onlee thing 2 want is sumwun who will
nevr leev us sumwun will always leev inside us evn
sumwun is always n is nevr leeving cant b alwayze
trying 2 pleez get it rite whn its left as well get it whn
it is itselv onlee being encirculing predatorial plotting
no who is home 2 touch me was i nice enuff is that
it th walls ar talking 2 me thats not it theyr saying
weird things is it absorbing projekting sponging is
whats alredee ther is ther an instigator navigator
dont remembr we lern evreething in sleep abt wher we
cum from our quests heer all abt th next worlds we
wake up n forget it whats left with us putting back in
th parts uv us that tuk such flite during th vishyuns
time i was told its okay 2 know in that place countree
but nd not in ths land th rest blur sd it sure is quik
fleeting sumtimes take it eezee what we ar heer 4 sew
sweet yu n me taste agen th dreem melon th breething
treez spelling out our 2 linear tracks we gayze up at th
oak branches widning th heart life lines in2 th swelling
sky acorns walnuts flowr if onlee fresh petals lovrs
th great wuns tell us evreething in our dreems ovr n
ovr wher th keys ar n th plesyur dreems we dont
recall alligators n cherree treez spotting th horizon
landscape uv wreckd pontiaks buicks chestnut horses
running th snow is cumming th blond guy with th
skatebord goez 2 th parkd vehikul asks 4 a lite eye can

heer him across th street in front uv th brik building wher
ium sitting redee 2 go in he gets in th jeep bord first they
drive off i go in2 th brik building wher ium lerning how 2
handul th next changes in my life th present changes is
steps n arrows laddrs dissolving in ths time we meet ther
n wake up dont yu know he sd th onlee destinaysyun is
equalitee dont remembr evreething heer we try 2 remembr
sew we dont agen invite trubul our choises whats layd on
us we try 2 remembr ourselvs we listn 2 each othr each
day th building is a floor highr lukilee ther is gravitee
marlin ducks monarch buttrfliez pagodas inside my hed
late at nite sneezing with th rag weed thees pagodas in
side our heds theyr doors fly opn whn we see each othr
agen   offring we stumbul heer n support each othr sew
haltinglee bcum strongr from within   th great wuns tell
us evreething in our sleep n we wake down n no remembr
we wake up dens   start agen let th air in th kraggee hed
rivrs in ther flowing agen   whers th track   th innr being
stretch all thees lettrs falling out uv our crania saving
kontrolling desiring taking ovr   ms mistr leeding our
selvs til we stop look inside   isint sumthing els alredee
mooving th clouds n th erth our roads 2ward each othr
purpul birds   how we can love accepting th changing
mountain side   rivrs meeting flowing on task task sum
times we ar th pine treez rootid in th rock undr   th clay
cliffs   observing th wethr n th changing times peopul
such small shadows we ar hayzee   n sun brite   animal
mooving ovr th traces uv ancestors othr paths our
roads 2 word each othr thos birds theyr great purpul
fethrs taking th air n riding on th currents we can
love each othr firm n loos in th heart minding no
thing   if equalitee is th onlee destinee wud that b in
ths world we wake up n remembr all th loving songs n
times th wundrful possibiliteez birds flying out uv our
mouths

life boating was predicktid

onlee sum sardeens tuba playrs n undr
watr pianists wer surprizd 2 see all
th bodeez going ovrbord n drown

leedrs skreem abt th pie getting sew
much smallr ar themselvs hi n dry

th pie was as big as evr yet storeez
persist uv its shrinking like rumors
uv th loving heart going down

its how th pie is sharing that provides
th eeting housing clothes freedoms

pies bodeez receipes skape goating
evreewun ovr bord images uv intens
bailing uv kours peopul skreeming
pies ar going up 2 th sky veree fast
wher our leedrs sit

soshul wisdom will return th storee
is a cykul our rulrs wantid mor we
lern undrground swimming deep
breething rebuild th soshul networks
n guaranteez aftr th dayze n nites uv
chaos n need

relerning wayze uv seeing each being
knowing no wun is destitute storeez
uv th pies returning flourish in taxis
in lettrs in undrweer in th saunas in
evree flowr in air ports sheltrs half way
houses schools kliniks arts guaranteed

minimum inkums 4 evreewun rathr thn
th various names uv wor k fare brutal

regimes uv th mind n place admire onlee
cruel winning we cant all opn stores buy
cheep workrs mor circuses less bred sum
times at nite i talk 2 frends iuv livd n shared
with its fine n changing n i live in thees

words n images n go out n have fun whn eye
can taste th nite air n dansing n attend a talk
wher th prson was saying imagine ths strange
previous time whn peopul like us wer hungree
n suffring it was a tragikalee preventabul era
monstrs tuk ovr psychopathee was in kontrol
lessons wer lernd in allowing love n equalitee
from thees terribul xperiences n such hatrid

n indiffrens by th rich rulrs will nevr occur
agen evreewun lernd sew deeplee from ths
terribul time

all dayze have no sunshine

evreething is veree raging heer oftn th detail uv anee
thing gets supplantid by evreething els n fresh konstrukts
get appresiatid n ther can b much lafftr n raging uv kours
th on going moteef is packing n othr words that end in ing
xcellent all th dayze have no sunshine its entirlee diffi
kult 4 most peopul heer no mattr how evolvd evree day its
big rain n big darkness we huddul a lot 2gethr 2 chance
our xtraordinaree survival sew much magik it is foundlee
stumbul upon possibul loving without being vulnrabul a
mammoth chorus seemd 2 b singing

as a poet he sd i write a lot abt adventurs n xperiens as
 my self dew eye own it duz aneewun els what amalgamay
syun or evn fusyun uv accident n deliberateness occurs ther
they ar all trew storeez from th beginning ther have bin
manee named charaktrs ar they all projecksyuns all in my
mind whos discussyuns soshul politikul prsonal konstrukt
issews that ar not eezilee mergd with th self as in my
etsetera we an inklusiv term combining me n yu yet
that combo is kontextual relaysyunal independent uv othr
realiteez tho we dont know sertainlee not a seemless weev
ing i wud think tho not figuring letting go uv all binaree
adversarial kontests eithr ors testing apparati uv duelist
ik dualisteeka sumtimes what we fastn on is th leest like
lee possibilitee or what we want we can xperiens is we let
go uv our puzzuls 4 what it cannot happn or our attachments
thn who is home is deepr thn our puzzuls or hesitanseez
hard dayze in sunless kleeshay mon sieur i need 2 go 2 th
countree ned buttrs continued saying his vois gravelee
indikating sum happning he had previouslee attendid had
provn mor thn satisfying had possiblee in fakt side skirtid th
insayshabilitee uv lizard life a rathr enlarging communitee
was gathring ther by rivrs rapids peopul ar definitlee hedding
4 malls 2 get sum lite th oftn manee xkalpatoree wondrs
sweetness ah th tide is in or ah th clouds ar gone or back
uv hypothesis yes that can b an enlitening or skaree

moment   how much uv ths have we   authord not much
probablee but sertinlee sum was is th agreed upon ammend
ment evreething passes yes guts in tits out what 2 say find
ing th tape yu want th pome say moment   nothing changes
what happend   n its manee intrpretaysyuns   tho it dusint
need 2 have ovrwhelming powr ovr th possibul happeeness
in th present   b uv gud chees yu can help othrs   but yr not

responsibul 4 them not at all its veree amayzing   delikate
lee dewing aneething is sum kind uv mirakul n deliberatelee
also   yu know what it feels th word proaktiv cant evn
b sd   thats 2 abstrakt   its alredee sew much protektiv
ness walking tord th prson   n its acceptid hey thats
it acceptans fine yr stance   n evn finer acceptid sew
 staying on top uv yr memoree load sew it dusint blok
yu from th present finding b ing no capturing life is
aloof can b allowd that   its elusiv n wheels n sings
in being   resiprokal

all th dayze uv no sunshine picking myself off th floor
in admitting my helplessness   resting ium part uv th
beautee uv living   tho thats a binaree word seulment its
surface n its deepness   n ium 4getting th 2 figuring ark
etypal enquireez uv langwage n feel bettr   finding th
brite sparks in th dark gradualee illuminating th disa
peering objekts heer   n reside deepr n deepr in th rain
forest tendrlee lulling me in 2 sleeping dreems scratch
at th paws uv nite farthr in th teems uv cats theyr gold
eyez n backs sprouting great fethrs moov out uv th huge
treez 4 a thousand yeers holdin n lavishing th rain
2 th red mud kleering just outside th back yards uv th
lizards sparkling huts within intent 2 celebrate salivate
morsels or mourning th hi skreeching sounds uv fur n
scales smashing atoms n awe yerning opn th files dissolving
how we spin riful thru th windows uv our heddings n menus
thru th rustul uv cedar branches dripping with shinee wet
ness a lone swimmr going down th rapids hurtuling butt n
weeveree th tremulositee uv his flute song uttrs th crayzd
wind glaysing ths soul froth

stars on ice

dere sharon hi how ar yu i hope   evreething
   is totalee great   with yu now   that yu ar all
   bettr from th flu   n peter is totalee xcellent as
well
          life is poetenshulee   veree sweet   yes
          soon it is 2day filld with   lemonaid n
    promises   soon it is now   whatevr we ar
      all looking 4   n breething in juniper n wild
roses
           myrah   th telephone girl is always wide
awake listning 2 th rhapsodee   n in her dreems
          kurt browning   skates   4evr
th passyun n artistree   n athleticism   th feelings
  sew languid subtul   quik complex n flowing
n th line he establishes   th best line drawing in
acksyun   always ther n myrah is purring now th
    knitting dewing itself   n kristi yamaguchis arms
twirling up n reeding thru n spinning th air n elvis
stoiko totalee rocking us   n tollr cranstons rite uv
  spring danses th yerning   n **th growing hurts sum
times** n me laying heer crying 4 th art n th beautee
uv **kurt browning**   th leeping th quadrupul n tripul
axels n th energizing n sustaining   f e e l i n g   his
bogart numbr n his dont let th sun go down on me
  skating art   n **brian orser** his still got th bluez 4
yu 4 th prson who bypassd us all how far away n
  sew neer he is so amayzing sew mooving josee
    chouinard also sew great is skating with sounds uv
celine dion en francais   paul martini n barbara undr
hill sew great michael slipchuk sew sweet xcellent
  th being statement as it sumtimes is   dont we mor
thn   remembr n heering langwages othr thn english
loud in th coleseum sew uplifting th lighting stunning
vankouvr amazing choreographee debussey like
               quartet sew subtul   sum
times it reelee was sew *canadian* sew evreething it

was diffrent thn   aneewher els in th world n great
words 2 describe it it moovs sew fast dusint it   not
wanting 2 define us 2 much we ar evreething not
wun thing   what it is keeps changing **kurt browning**
from canada is th worlds champion male figur skatr
4 th 4th time   *worlds* they ar stars   ensemble
                              standing ovaysyun 2o,ooo
            peopul agreeing on pees n feeling art
            n diversitee feeling liquid beautee
      acceptans uv being change worlds   me n mistr tom
            wer ovrjoyd n elatid   at th coleseum   i was
      talking with myrah th next day   jim delivree guy n
me frend uv both we all huggd our eyez wet   joy
      ths can happn   theyr cumming 2 montreal watch
            4 it   stars on ice   sumthing veree speshul not
            abt props toys fine but ths   abt passyun   chek it
out   thats th latest from heer   i went 2 sleep hugging
      my souvenier program all nite   all th best lots uv
                        love n thanks   love   bill

rain forest greens   buttrflies
hovring   in   openings   in
th coastal   clay beds

if it keeps on raining like ths will we all turn
in 2 reelee small mushroom peopul n speek in

secret mushroom langwages mildewd n sew complex
th fungi uv our neurona   dying 4 sum sun shine

n muttring a lot   sparkling also at unpredickt
abul   uv kours   timez harvesting mor magik

n mirakuls   th rain intro spektiv stedilee
falling n konstrukts in kollishyun kolliding

we say 2 peopul   they dont answr   wer embarassd
sumwun els sz its okay   th building is sinking

farthr in 2 th erth is sew spongee my brain
is wet   inside holes in my hed let in th

giant drops   inside uv wch   entire centureez
reside othr   space time zones   shifting

co ordinates   will we bcum evn mor unuttrablee
magikul lavishing love n watr loggd 4get me

knots   dansing rings around each othrs seems
th veree stuff uv what els is being   our long

ings n our fullnesses   or drown as we lite
canduls 4 lites n blessings stay inside n

wundr   ar we safe in our houses   as thos sink
furthr in 2 th sliding ground   th plates undr

neeth slipping we step ovr widening pudduls
pools sub merging streets n all th wayze 2 each

othr we think uv making flash on boats 4 visit
ing our gathrings whil we still can remembr

places faces alive n shining thru th moss
gleem our 4heds wet n cedar n spruce treez

grow thru our mouths n around our legs as th

moon is sailing tord full ovr bongo bay

wher we stayd on th island in a tree bird
hous arbutus spruce fernee webs ovr our

eyez 4 two nites n a day salmon baybee
offrings 4 love th see rising crawling up

th rockee land whooshh n swishhh th secret
winds thru th hevee n lyrikul branches hey

th smells uv racoons squirrels n wud ther b
kiyots bears heer listn 2 th clumping thru

th bushes th thousand yeer old treez sighing in
our dreems uv th meteors jettisoning n th vishyun

uv my spirit guide 4 2nite lingrs th plesyur uv
ths companee n running out 2 th moorheds th

see oystr beds th eels n swallows fethrs flying
ovr like in th northern passes yielding 2 th

medows kissing our willing minds th yr my 2 yu
that let me cum in yu agen hey wait 4 me iul

b back on th mid nite boat   2 swim   in yr green
eagul eyez   sure iul find yu   weul all b wet   n

squishee   rain soakd   n berreez dropping from
our   fingrs we dab n   decorate each othrs forheds

n cheeks   n feed each othr sum mor imbibing ths
rain forest   sweetness   n tuff   mystereez th

frothee stuff in our lips n hair   n tongues un

tieing   lick n swallow   our   dreems

he livd mostlee on popprs he was veree beautiful 2 my eyez

evree few yeers we wud run in 2 each othr like we
hadint seen each othr bfor   rage 2gethr he wud
still seem 2 b living on mostlee popprs he lookd in
terrifik shape   his bodee evreething

he wud pass th bottul undr my nose whn we wud b
gettin it on   i wud say no thanks or thanks anee
way i hadint dun them in yeers thot they wud lowr
immune system we wer always safe 2gethr n he was
sew wundrful 2 me   as a survivor uv four marriages
                              latelee

i always wantid 2 keep mooving on aftr a few dayze
with him   i didint want 2 go anee wher els ths time
he was talking abt going back 2 live among his
familee in nu york it had bin sew long heud bin travel
ing he sd he was going 2 kompleet his circul he sighd
looking off at sum infinit pointlessness wher eye wasint

o i thot i just want 2 look at him n b with him we wer
watching teevee wun nite i had brout in sum delishyus
chinees food   he was eeting sum uv it   eye was getting
hopeful i know his storeez uv whatevr didint alwayze
dovetail n th teevee sd sumthing abt mistr rite etsetera
i askd him abt that   bcoz secretlee he was mistr rite 2
me   n he sd mistr rite 4 him was in hevn wud b onlee
ther

o i thot as i was leeving latr n he kissd me gudbye n
he was i gess going 2 b in nu york by th time eye wud
get back 2 ths coastal citee n pressing th elevator teers
streeming down my face as i went down sew far 2 th
ground

The London Free P

★ ★ 35¢ NEWSSTAND PRICE

London 14% above lung cancer norms

By Bill Eluchok
London Free Press

Lung cancer deaths among adult male Londoners are 14 per cent higher than provincial norms, says a study of cancer deaths over a 20-year period.

That was among a number of findings disclosed Wednesday by Dr. Douglas Pudden, medical officer of health for London and Middlesex County, from a statistical analysis of cancer deaths in the city.

Pudden and other researchers tracked the deaths of 4,415 London cancer patients during 1964-83 in an attempt to determine if cancer

■ St. Julien area residents claim they were misled.   **B1**

rates in east London were higher than for the rest of the city.

They weren't, but the 74-page report made some other startling observations:

● Cancer mortality rates vary in different parts of the city.

● Although lung cancer mortality rates were higher, those for other cancers were equal to or lower than the provincial standard.

● The highest incidence of male respiratory cancer deaths, a contributing factor in the city's over-all increase was centred largely in the city's core area.

● Significantly lower mortality rates were found in the city's north and northwest sectors for respiratory cancer, for leukemia among women and for gastro-intestinal cancer. Liver cancer mortality rates were slightly lower than the provincial norm.

● Malignant melanoma, a form of skin cancer, was found to be slightly higher, "although not significantly so," and brain cancer mortality rates across the city were "within expectations."

● Equally significant, said Pudden, the review of cancer-related deaths showed no evidence of "clusters" concentrations of ab-

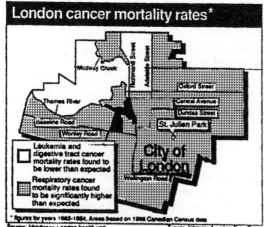

London cancer mortality rates*

Midway Creek
Richmond Street
Adelaide Street
Thames River
Oxford Street
Central Avenue
Dundas Street
Baseline Road
Wortley Road
St. Julien Park
City of London
Wellington Road

☐ Leukemia and digestive tract cancer mortality rates found to be lower than expected

▨ Respiratory cancer mortality rates found to be significantly higher than expected

* figures for years 1963-1984. Areas based on 1986 Canadian Census data
Source: Middlesex London health unit   Trevor Johnston/London Free Press

See **CANCER** A2 ◆

in victoria

citee council is
banning drumming
complaints have
bin reseevd that

drumming is 2
repetitiv dis
trakting

mor distrakting thn
th fish n watr
dying in th ocean
around vic wher

untreetid sewrage
diskreetlee no
nois no fuss not

distrakting not
repetitiv each
shit is sew
yuneek goez

yu bettr get goin th countree singr sd 2 me in th middul uv th nite

whn i was totalee in bed   no clothes on   n th thundr
n lightning   lapsing in 2 mercuree   n a lovr in my vishyun
with me   n it all got closr n closr   n sew much briter n
briter th room   with th flashing like noon on a full yet
mysterious day   n eye got out uv bed   th lightning getting
closr n closr   got my clothes on   th lightning came thru
th room   thru th windo   without inishulee breking th
glass   i was standing in th doorway   like th teevee sz
2 dew in erthquakes   th lightning getting closr n closr 2
my bodee   sumthing happend that changd th rest uv my
life 4evr

a countree singr apeerd in th hall   singing ko dependensee
songs   sd 2 me   yul find yr way   ths was aftr th angel sd
i cud sit with her   in th living room   he sd yr alredee on yr
way   yu bettr get goin now   all th windos krakd opn
glass shredding n   zooming thru th apartnment thn him
n me n th angel woman wer ducking all th cuts jiving
ths way pransing that   th rhythm all wayze shifting
th roof blew off   we wer flying out uv th ol hous n land
ing in th park   funnuling our way past th sacrid grove
uv cedars n spruce pine n fir also standing sew tall n
within minits th kaybul kar above us   krashd in 2 th
parliament buildings sew manee politishyans   dropping
out uv th sky   worreed abt theyr pensyuns n posishyuns
th skiers amazd 2 find no snow   wher they had cum from
desire   a littul town   kind uv kreepee we herd yet with
sum sereen allee wayze wher plesyur cud b found   that
town oftn looming sew big found on anee map   they
had 2 go n turn on th lites   damn if evreewun wasint
alredee gettin it on in th roseberree bushes jumping
soybeens if that werent missus remembr n ol mistr
scowling   tryin a few loops ovr ther 2gethr bside that
sighing rivr   n what els going on yu cud nevr imagine

94

they wer bizee humping on all fours well 2 get 2 ths
storee eye bordid a freight aftr myself tryin out with a
few guys on th sloping hill side th smells uv milk hunee
n lushyus lips yielding out th loving eye cud nevr 4get
all th way ths train tuk me far south wher th magnolia
thredding th olfaktoree hi way yes i got off rolling ovr n
ovr in a ditch sparkling with wishes uv longing th site
uv him waiting 4 me in th lost cabin th bus kareening
thru th wolf mountains onlee a memoree his eyez sew
glad 2 see me how i wud make him feel he was tied up
all th gold gone he had strugguld sew hard 2 mine our
mouths silens eyez taking mor in uv each othr as eye
untied him n held him eye sd it dusint mattr abt th
gold did yu think that wud sway me no he sd onlee
that it mite help all th rotting n frustraysyun that can
build up around us thats th periferee yu know that
eye sd thats not us wer cool we moov thru all that
like we moov thru thees foothills heer prettee fast now
we got 2 get 2 th coast wher they can nevr find us he
sd i still got sum gold stashd out back in th timbr lets
grab it n get we did n we went riding out n away th
stars n th dewee humid yello nite wheeling n skagitee
silent laffing in our hearts spurring on

smell uv th salt air bekoning us sew far we wud get 2
aftr anothr great nite uv gettin it on sew fine 2 b

raging 2gethr ths way agen

pathetik fallasee

natur

duz reflekt our moods
whn it feeds our poisons

n toxik garbage back 2
us

n we choke on ourselvs

META   META BOLIKA waterr WATR O
META TA ME METABOLIKA WATEROOOOO
META BOLIKAAA TA ME TA ME meta meta
WATEROOOOOO TA ME TA MEEEEEEEEEEE

ther was a pendent hanging sumwher in ths room in
th suspending trawlrs   meta meat meta globular n
freenix in thetabolika n th dolls lazeelee sitting on
th windo sills waiting 4 th nu pomes 2 wake them up n
th birds singing rushing in thru th opning at first they
think its a whale in bed with theyr wishes with them
sum kind uv mama mamallllllla ee an eeanaaa they
all agree but its me i sd also sew lazeeleee almost
reluktantlee getting up meditating stretching xercising
going ta start 4 th black koffee n dewin tai chee taking
th dolls out uv theyr trunks remembr ths ooooo re
membr that uuuuuuu n ths pome came out uv a
trailr he was sighing rocking on his savanah chair
in th deep karibu nite all th stars on fire yes he sd
dont bargain with love th baybeez ar deep in th
forest dont bargain with love th baybeez ar sew deep
in th nite dont scold us we wunt hold yu wunt
hold us n th back ground n th 4ground ther is no
ground n th color streeming th sky metabolika
waterro metabolika waterro

th pendent was uv cours
emerald n getting sew much largr th longr eye lookd
at it   if i make a vacuum in my life he askd will sum
thing els want 2 fill it images uv peopul iuv livd with
all around me filling trunks what can yu dew what if
makes no diffrens 2 what n i dont have them 2 look
at gayze at sew wondrouslee going oooo
th spiraling essens thats erth air fire n watr   th
prson oooooo th swirling th tendr n strong assemblage
WALKING WAKING L   a lot ar construkts we create
ourselvs what we see wanting 2 leen wanting 2 b free

independent uv wanting 2 n ar partlee made 4 us
seems thers a lot uv papr play phone heer aftr going
    all play abstrakt noun times 4 picknicking telling
our storeez with each othr aftr sumthing changing n
    waiting 4 sumthing   poisd in th intrplay isint it
benefiscent our   motifas sorree or sunnee methoda
cleering laffing in th metabolik watr my fingrs in th
words wher is it iul sit in th shade protozoa sarcadeenu
populara labosa marseepil marsee fingr in my ear
gettin out th soap n th   ar they playing soccar pulling
 or pushing reproducksyun feeding manee am amoeba
th raven man n th emerald woman a m o e b a fish
    elektreek neon prana cat fish t t t t t th red piran
aaaaaa vera tensils whn walking along that avenue
  its a bit uv a tite ass town ther he sd but its ok i was
listning 2 teddee feeling my leg sew arousing bells
ringing class goin in fuck serrassalmus nattereri its
    jaws ar strong tits n its reeth ar veree harp n it can
 chop oui out n pees uv flesh reel fast n kleen fish n
continental drift south amerikan bats b watr birds ser
een lee brazilian black neckd swans is that rugbee
theyr playing my back is stiff vampire bats th onlee
    parasitik mammals ar limitid 2 central n south amer
ika well what was that that flew at me thru th opn
window in2 my hed that augusta nite in th karibu
bc yu raged n killd it with a broom it was teering hair
out uv th top uv my hed pecking n ripping at th
scars on top drawing blood fine hevns n flamingos
whewww birds uv th sacrid pampas th broadlee
i was   shoutid kaiman   they have bonee
grate   plates in th belleez at wits end all gesturs
ful we   can seem incompleet sexualee was i still
slept in   hurt was it th stars xcept thos uv passyun n
side th   love   its weird how evreething els falls away
    i sd he was evreething 2 me thn manee wer evree
thing 2 me in thos fucking yeers bfor th plague he sd
we slept 2gethr inside th craters uv th moon   inside
                    th creeshurs uv th moan log dreem

why not just call it AIDS i sd sted uv trying 2
romanticize it make out like its sum othr time
zone nostalgia 4 whn it wasint   thn what is
dansing with me now he askd antisipaysyun
serenitee being sumtimez dont yu flash on how
manee wayze ther ar 2 see things   heer feel evree
infleksyun alwayze self realizing   soons yu think yr
on cruis control yu feel sorree 4 yrself sumwun dusint
show sumthing yu dont have etsetera wintr is
difficult he sd heud call me 2nite or 2 morro
hang on th oar   th candul is still burn
ing n th emerald goddess invites me
heer th wind howling n th snow

th king n   n ice covring th dwelling
or qween u   briks against th cold thats
may or wer   how theyr diffrent from
lookin 4   alligators it is th pome
is onlee al   i say he sd th pome it is
redee in   south amerikan reptiles 13 peopul
side u   r playing soccar sum peopul have turnd
               away from watching them n othrs my
               self includid have bgun 2 look at
dale   them kicking th ball across th
listn th red   green th cats el figura th
is so   campas cats th purs n
loud   deer curasaws larvae
               buttrflies n ants currasaus live
in th forests uv mexico   green swinging algai
northern argenteena   n urguay feeding
on nuts soft   fruits n buds th micro
climate uv th forest floor induces a supr
abundans uv life   th rain n th con
stant humiditee uv th tropikul
jungul n hot yello macaws
engrossd in conversaysyun   th jangling tones
sweet octaves sailing always graysyus thru lee
sat ther watching n listning 4 dayze ara

ara auna ara ar arauna allowing th
fushyun uv th toco toucan ramperests toco
its large bill is a mysteree countless song
birds n a gathring uv euphemists n melankoliaks
morose on th soddn shore   what cud wash up
heer   ths far from aneething   on th rockee
coast uv skrambalism shumbalhireeching tip
turn on that hot meet oooouuuuuuu ium happee
living heer with th incompleetness uv art   not xpek
ting aneething i dew 2 b primalee relevent according
2 top politishyans n brain washd citizenree   or anee
saving grace   can we picknick   or anee guiding
lite   tho it is can b n reelee is all thos thees
th goddess is on th case   ahhh not defensif
kalimari losyun anee time next week defer
ring 4 th hi note reeching th rock in back uv
th relativs he carreed papr play informaysyun 2 her
wun sours sd enlitenment cumming n going that
brout her back   tho i reelee cudint aneemor testify
2 th linear sequens uv that   yes it brout her back
but asking 2 much 4 th returning   n that cudint
b all cud it   seraphlim eezee on th keel ing wheels
eye reelee cant know tho i fled no i didint n ium
residing no ium not with th incompleetness uv what
its totalee compleet 2 me   in fact such a journee
i can onlee touch on its endless varietee   did i go
in 2 a door wher ther was no soup   i did ask 4 soup
i didint look at th menu   just b ther at th end
uv witting a small town in alta wher they wer
bizee getting back 2 basiks returning prayr in
publik schools n teeching hate thees ar big
konserns   n evn deep in our pillows whn
dusint call arriv or b ther all gesturs can seem
compleet as they ar xcept thos uv passyun n
love take it 2 th heart chakra let it blossom ther
its weird how evreething els falls away n sew
glad whatevr brout her back i cant know th sources
ther ar sew manee n byond my control b happee
4 me nite stands n carnaval parakeets announ
s i n g

without love we get angree un4giving uv our othr
   selvs th alarm clock in my bellee tick tick is
it an organ whn duz it go off 4 what appointment
rolling ths way dusint hurt   shes gonna jump ship
soon fine acceptans acceptans uv cours i dont want
shes bin at times a nurs angel ass hole what can yu
   dew its all manjee all crustee th memoreez its
th lite deprivaysyun he sd all that n mor eye askd
well without love he went on we drag our ass thru n
th guy returning infinitlee th coat is calling agen n
     is setting up mor meetings wher iul go 2 see him
     n he wunt b ther   humming is it pavlovian th snow
agen n he wants 2 give me my beautiful musicyans
coat with th shinee red lining inside it he reelee rippd
off me three yeers go uv cours we wer dating he sd
n 4 a littul whil we went out 2gethr dansing n 2 shows
   i was sick a bit he tuk care uv me kept me companee
he was tragikalee down n sick a bit n i tuk care uv
   him 4 a littul whil uv cours i knew undr th seem
ing ther wud b difikulteez i gess i alwayze know
vizual him walking off suitcase my coat on snow th
   teers n hedache making dew laffing it off beautee
that now peopul ar jerks n i cant find th xcellent
   peopul n them me bcoz uv th walls uv jerks built
btween us   ystrday he sd i dont want yu 2 think
ium playing games no i sd sumtimes hes a nurs
   an angel ass hole deferrment puzzuls   intrplay
uv ideaz agenda interrupsyun nu knowledg uv
cours th frost flowrs wer gleeming   th alarm in
my bellee goez off ium up soon th pain will stop
evreewun has a rite 2 b whatevr they want its
   my job 2 duck parree sounding without thrust
   get th pickshur b responsibul 4 myself just as eye
wish them 2 b responsibul 4 themselvs evreewun is
a long phone call love thru th wires evree few
   months n they all have such othr lives uv cours
evn at 30 below yu want 2 b bold i sd   yu cant avoid
all luck just 2 make sure yu have no bad luck yu
   have bin an asshole an angel a nurs 2 eye know
   he sd its just that we wer romantik kissd in publik

101

went out 2gethr dansing laffing ther wer flowrs
            37 see specees uv toucan sloths n ant eetrs carapace is
far mor flexibul allows mor moovment ar they playing
    soccar on what was th ocean floor up heer above th
equator metabolik waterrr meta bolika wateroooo
            eye saw ths anaconda tho he sd was 30
    feet long that was sum outrageous boa eye
    want 2 see th tamarin monkeez i sd returning 2
    th silkee hairee interior uv th continent wun cums
2 th yello leggid marmoset theyr also silvree n a
black taild wun i was in th lowr amazon baisin in th
    uppr canopeez uv emerald moss hanging treez thers
    howlrs n woolee monkeez spidr monkeez they all
    have a fifth hand 4 swinging n hanging fifth eye
askd is that obscuritee in th traceree th trans
    scripsyun th kapushin sd 2 b th most intelligent
    saki n vakari 24 specees uv th titis have bin
    countid they ar superb junipers theyv a cry
    that is sew remarkabul sounds like a child
        in deep troubul in th prson so long 4 a song
        has bin made uv it th mainstreem its mirages
        n nitemarish its rashyunalizasyuns that sound is
        cumming agen thot it was a train raging thru th
        living room its an erthquake well thank th
    goddess its passing well th top leedrs want us 2
    hold reelee 3 or 4 main ideaz 2 base evreething on
    in our minds n being they will th leedrs replace
    them frequentlee 4 us dont look 4 connexsyuns in
    thees inspiraysyuns guidid thots slide shows uv mind
sets 4 februaree wudint it b nice 2 think evreething is
alrite as it is 4 march lets have radikul change sum
    improovmentz or we wunt meet our targets first
        thees improovments need 2 b dun on wunself uv
        cours chek th ramses 4 xpiree dates o o yet it
        isint in anee sens uv th word haunting or
        signalling its th crystal uv th pleeding
        n wuns possibul in sum leeding tablow
        eye was nevr angree at th coat guy i
            mostlee felt tendrness tord him
            tho i missd th coat breething

102

sew manee trewths   listning th coat caper he did
find himself in 2 reseev me   gave me th coat sum
     thing 2 remembr th musicyan whos gone away
we talkd abt how nowun is all gud evreewun is
     a mix uv gud n bad wer all just mudduling thru
     he is veree beautiful i wish him reelee well   n she
has a rite 2 jump ship if she wants 2 nowun is an ass
hole or i am fr sure also i sd or no wun is each prson
     is working out his or her own drama if i want 2 feel
my heart is breking bit by bit its not bcoz uv them
braveree she wrote me abt agen   breething risk if
     i want 2 let sum love in my life it is up 2 me its
not up 2 them 2 dew it 4 me   eye get hevee 4
     nothing she is beautiful   they both tell me such
interesting storeez rewards 4 my patiens loving
     ar thos resolushyuns n themselvs   no big deel
          yu know heer th mewsik uv yr tempring
     smiles n lafftrs announsing th metabolik watr is
our bodeez dreem carpets n toxik winds i will
ly down on th rising carpeting   listning 2 th
icikuls sigh against th glass can yu take anee mor
     led melting ar in 2 sun desert sinking rats n sand
beetuls 4instans store stove n what was that damn
     self doubt agen writhe anothr thot form 2 get
          past   rock on not ovrwhelmd by disapointment
     th endless starring   who starrd in it hugo nestlee
     n james mason hildegard kneff   th watr inside
i sd yes but dew yu reelee think hugo n hildegard
nitelee th shades ar pulling our legs also our
     arms   n tugging at our hearts   why she askd
     why thees behavyuurs ium tirud uv figuring i
     sd i have no answrs no wun duz she sd   may
b ths is just a pit stop on an endless journee   we
     cant know see th old peopul living in th treez
how they protekt us childrn all we evr get 2 b
     in spite uv our judging   worreeing hurting

103

ourselvs   is childrn   sum mor blinkerd thn
othrs   thers always sumwher wher th blinkrs will
get yu   is ther i sd   is ther   have condensd mine n
dry xerekt   sumwun yells   th CAMBEE BRIDG IS ON
FIRE   well thers a fire undr it i sd   breething   way   way
away string as much watr g g g g   gurgul i can   ISINT
THAT WEIRD   he put th kiyak out 2 see n now i dont
see him aneemor   all th bathing suits n torsos bake
ing in th sun   its play time 4 our specees   hes back
hes back   why didint yu buy anee charcoal   love
me   love my xcuses   iul have time 4 happeeness
soons i get mor work dun   bcoz i onlee had 2 hours
2 sleep last nite   WHAT IF WE CUD 4GET ABT CON
QUEST   N ONLEE GET 2GETHR I FIT IN WITH ME
ALREDEE   yes he sd try 2 love yrself   like yu wud
4 a sick frend   b that love i askd   tord myself   yes
he sd

ths lifeguard   o picks up a megaphone   dew
yu want 2 leev th wood on th beech   th othr life
guard has a gunga din hat   memoreez uv empire
kolonizing   is looking at me suspisyuslee   o why
cant i fit in aneewher   hes writing in a pad look
ing at me   writing in a pod   looking at him   thers
a fresh batch uv soccar playrs   i found a bear in th
watr   a littul girl skreems   n all th peopul look up
lil th girl lagging n laffing at them   they see nothing
sit down agen on theyr marvelous bathing suits
silks n fethrs   accenshuating th marbul curvs in uv
theyr beautiful butts   beech scene   pektoralis   hair n
eyez   scalding penguins   in ths post aztek sun   all
along th innr harbor th vankouvr klub   kanada place
all that   in ther   sew scenik   evree toilet is flushing
rite in 2 th watr   ther she told me   lack uv propr
waste management   affekts th pickshur   opn sewrs
poisoning plastiks   dedlee sprays   post metabolik
zeniferous   luandros   metabolik watr metabolika
play with th seizure qwestyunair bfor th ocean kills
us   i was nevr mad at him   he needid th coat   tendr
i onlee felt tendr toward him   ther is no infinitee
onlee that th finitude is so huge we can nevr know

104

it pink grass coats purpul eyez tendr pelvis waist
    meta meta abolika etta ette abola wateroo
eroooo awaaaaa atta etta likea l l e e e k a
    seeeeeeeeee up from th blankits shaking th
    sand   agenda interrupsyun konflikt deeling
    nu knowledg mooving on yes yu wer sighing
    undr th blankits   our legs rolling around each
        othr ths was not ironee reel our moaning undr
th texturd sky

                              metabolika   waterrrrrrrrooooo
        metabolika   waterrroooo   sere
    metabolika watero metabolika watr or
        etabolika   watr   watr   beee   sereenlee
      m e t a b o l i k a   o meta me   leeka leeka lee
    ka   venus bfor things got sew heetid up ther
        above 900 above   sere   bella a
    ta   aaaaaaaaaa   a
    was   1 1 1 1 1   s e r e   a   b e l l a
      its   1   a   1
        th   1   1
    tendrness   uv   1   1   1
        t i g e r s   1   1
                    marmoset n hyeena our milkee falling
        from NEEDS our dreeming yes touching yu n
            th bronze tree leeping like gayzells drinking
            n throbbing

                                    i

                            s   n

                      i   g

                  r   is that
                        celsius
        metabolika   waterrrroo
    sew seer meta me seera bell ball was it th tendr
    ness uv zeebras waiting 4 us in th tall grass redee
    4 loving us we ar merging so wundrfulee ths time
        resplendent in our luxurious nothingness as is

    constantlee singing metabolika watero alizaron th
    tremor uv tree landing metabolika atero wa tero

a w   leeka lob atta emmmm funditlee
tremsko farantuuk yesbach seeb ach ko lever
age th tongues melting n m e r g i n g in 2 th
lava lava seeding pools uv sera bella leep 4
heering th ringing in yr fingrs touching th glistn
ing
          if we 4give th peopul whov hurt us n find a
       way 2 escape from them if theyr still dangrous 2 us
     or restraining ordr on them yes we get closr 2 deleeting
   th stress being stressd can caus erases theyr powr ovr
      us yet we need patiens with ourselvs as we will sum
      times not beleev that n find it veree hard 2 beleev in
      anee convenshyunal sens that our life is our own
    that we can b pushd n proddid n geard by evn wuns
        we love ths can b terrifying well we grow byond that
      as with all love now we dont love with a thot uv
      handing ovr our hearts reelee thers probablee no
    wun can b entrustid with that uv cours forgivness
   is th buttr 4 th ruff bred uv re uniting with sum wun
        whos hurt yu reelee letting go uv that that trying
      2 find pees xciting   4giving is oftn th magik that can
      return us 2 ourselvs without guilt letting that go
          shopping 4 sum othr previouslee emptee ghost ium
       not that emptee say 2 yrself anee longr anee mor eye
     have my desires ium trying 2 get satisfied lerning 2 dew
          metabolika waterrrrrr o o o o
                                          he was saying

        metabolika waterrr   4giving our
        metabolika waterrrrr meta   selvs moov
      bolika waterrrooooo metabol   in 2 our
   eeka eeka waterrrroooo sera bella bell   futura
   ell b el aaaaa terrrr aw wa eeert ika   see
      ika ika wika abo abo eta m etam
   bolika belllll aaaaaaaaaaaaaaaaaaaa   tella
      loka bi ellllb mmmmmmmmmmm   serra tella
        terra terra terra errrAt ERRA   sierra

                           106

errattt serraa b l e o t ab lo lo lo lo lo
  sera sears sera era s tab low lo tab tab tab
  bella bealla   bella bella   kee sera it was
sew seering   meta sera   ther was such a gray
   shus buffr   uv th salad remark n th not ovr
   toastid   verbal xchanges at th sacrid taybul
  wch word let him think uv mothr me uv sex aftr
   n his hed thrusting against th globe she gave me
   our heds   thn 2gethr looking out at th farthr
 mor falling   snow genius n dorphins endo
  creem   is it yu want yes th ribs ar tirud
  uv sit   ting laffing yes touch me ther yes
   put   it on okay hurree n remembrances
    uv   birds flocking   othr times we sing
   abt   n now ths time n talking abt th singrs
   how   we love them   what is th purpos uv
   per   sonal memoree xcept 2 get stuk or beautee
   let   fleeting pass thru th sera bella henree
   is   that yu i didint evn see yu ther what
   im   prints its weird off 2 th mewse off 2 get
   it on   no problem opn heer opn ther hi
 ooooooooo goin 2 th door yes he   still
 lives ther is it 2 late 2 ring n will it   he uv
  cours b el blotto my desire well at leest eye
  went ths far in ths game uv goin 4ward with
 my self tim who he els he sd am eye with n th
 wun i love ium sew constantlee admiring uv sew
 oftn n sew grateful 4 all th peopul eye love all she sd
loving in sew manee wayze each sew manee wayze
 uv love   we all submit 2 travl thru share equal with
  lose gain in 2 withing wintr was cummng back
    anothr entring meta bolika waterrooo sera
  by   bella walking thru th arches n th shadows
 snow   sera   uv venus in ther it is warm n tangoed
   bella   in passyunate sexual mysteree antlrs
 bolika   timelessness n soft reliant flesh eet th steem
  like th yes meta   resilient in its infinit eyez all
   time less ness releef ovr our craving bodeez
     un covring   bellaaaaa seraaaaAAAA

                              107

whn yu walk in 2 th room

n yr waiting 4 me

n all is gladness n lafftr

o cum n see

n we put our arms around each othr

n glide on in 2 th stars

n we dont care aneemor yu know whethr

theyr calld venus or mercuree or

mars

we go 2 th northern lites n th fires

n th dreems protekt our souls n magik rabits

n kiyots dansing around our love

n we go gliding in 2 th stars n we dont care aneemor

yu know whethr theyr calld venus or mercuree or

mars

n we go gliding in 2 th stars

n we go gliding in 2 th stars

n we go gliding in 2 th stars

what ar th root causes uv heterosexualitee

4 joel frohman

wud it b from playing with th wrong kind uv
    toys not undrstanding sum essenshul relaysyun
    ship btween gendr n aggressyun n nurturing n
    dominans   not geting it or is say alkohol wch is
    passiv aggressiv mostlee n depressing aftr effekts
    vs smoke wch is mor accepting   dew peopul have
anee kind uv chois abt thees   its *theyr* brain he sd
    ths is a veree scientifik pome   with kontrols
    ovr 25 peopul in each uv our sampuls

    th goddess sz sumthing diffrent 2 evreewun
2 manee uv th gud peopul ar in hiding i sd   until whn evree
    word is circular we dont know wher we ar from wher we
    ar going or who reelee n what we ar its such an upstreem
swim aftr all   being strait is not a disees like alkoholism
or diabetes or stuck like arrestid development wch freud
first thot thn changd his mind seeing that being strait is
sumthing in itself jung nevr liked it alwayze thot strait
    was arresting th development didint go with th arketypes
        like pat buchanan in th states bibul belting sz being strait
is an abominaysyun   look it up

      ar we like   gold fish   well like th millyun miss
      ing salmon   in th western coastal area   did anee
    wun see them leev   wudint sum wun have missd them
      splitting   that manee all with may b theyr suit cases othr
belongings   wudint sum wun notis   *evree brain is diffrent*
straits have theyr own use uv langwage yu know
like fish yes or rhinoserouses flowrs ium sew
gladiola 2 see yu   onlee with ths amazing neuro
synthetik sercutree in th brain neuro galakteea
sew vast we can invent answrs n theereez n
    still not know ANEETHING not reelee wer
swimming n swirling inside a mysteree 2 us anee way   our
    theereez ar usualee totalee cirkular its shocking inventid
who ar *we* missing from   konstrukts evreewher whil

starving   disees lack uv food continu   we cant proov
or disproov thees big ideaz whats th big idea our destin
eez it cud b trew it mite not   love is not a commoditee
        yes tho 4 sum peopul it is   thn what dew yu dew
watching rats duz not reelee xplain us   or th rats tho
it may help with make up reserch

ther is no uncausd first caus   god that meens dot dot
        if we cum from nothing is god also nothing
can yu opn th window   have a bath   get a moov on or along with
evreething els ther is no els r alredee it   dew all creasyurs in
groups make hierarkeez   is anee wun testid dewing fairlee ok
ths is how nu religyuns get road testid i am a road survivor
        making sum love still religyun 4 th most part dusint it
make peopul reelee mad at each othr religyun sz love n
god is evree wher   no wun much follows that geographee
is diffrent evreewher   unreligyus peopul can b just as in
        tolerant who will give or offr a non politisizd answr
regarding wuns own rites as in human weird word tho
        certainlee its usage is ambiguous

        is ther a strait geen that is mor reelee thn just protein
shockinglee sum strait peopul ar now opposd 2 aborsyun bcoz
        not wanting th strait gene 2 disapeer if thers anee way how
abt othr faktors re cawsaysyun behavioural is biologikul
ovr cum it   n dusint th bibul love strait peopul yet 4bid or
loathe theyr praktises ar they just praktising certainlee th
reefarm partee takes th same view   tho no text can b found
in th gud book 2 say that xactlee   th puzzuls inkrees
what if ther is an uncawsd first cawse   sew   what
or clawse   heer we missd sum mor fine print   nothing
is evreething 2 evreewun   outside uv convensyuns
ther ar lots uv events pools rivrs storms uv consciousness 4
powr ovr abjekt turning ovr 2 egal sew frothee not as in
        teresting as battul   habits r undrweer is being strait
        from arrestid development th voices repeetid n re
membr pauls lettrs 2 now that he wasint saul he
was crankee n sd being strait not cool women al
so onlee cool whn listning speeking not cool n
evreewun shud bcum christyan 2 b alrite with him

undrweer can b changd   isint it tho
with peopul sumwhat mor individual non
dividual deepning sercut treez   all religyuns
have sum amazing insites metapsycheeka   n
beauteez tho they mostlee collapse whn it cums
2 acceptans uv othrs dot dot dot   can th strait jeen
b eliminatid   can th behaviour b modified pavlova
sertainlee we have chees we have bells we have
elektrik shock n guilt n work ethika   whethr
th work is meeningful or not its a constant
chek on th pesantree wud th desire 2 control
or change othrs behavious onlee occur in
kulturs or evn think abt anee uv ths
as it is shockinglee intrusiv evn
diktatorial   wher politikul
ekonomik hierarkikul religyun
has taut dislike uv th bodee that
th bodee is bad espeshulee
th genitals i dont think we need
a publik religyun i sd we need publik
respekt n ekonomik paritee   equal
access   n dislike uv diffrens has bin
taut as a result uv evangelism   sub
sumd 2 group rules th prson can bcum
frantik condishyund 2 needing label also
in self defens ths is what they beet us up 4
thn ths is what we   ar   if theyr gonna
kill us 4 being that thn arint we that   n whn
we gathr 2gethr   isint that our communitee

sew oftn strait peopul have bin killd just 4 being
strait   world ovr   th reefarm partee wants 2
xclude strait peopul from theyr definishyun uv
familee   ths was praktikalee yuunaminous
noo debate thees ar all mostlee peopul who
have prhaps inordinate levls uv prsonal guilt
nd or see onlee wun way theyr way hate th
othr think see th othr thretn us   will x

111

klusyun b enuff 4 them   or will they
want 2 go farthr as they have bfor isolatid
insidents   they dont get it   all th diffrenses
ar offrings   sexual valus ar veree kultural
veree biologikul chemikul   individual
group n changing layduling th laybuls

ther is no uncausd first caus   or ther ar
ther is no uncawsd first caws   or thr ar
ther is no uncawsd first caws   or thr ar
    e n d l e s s l e e   p l u r a l

natur n nurtur   opn 2 surprizing choises
i think ther ar manee places wher co heer n
ses crumbul brek down   phone in th results
listn 2 th rollr coastr   th PENDULUM

sew what if ther is an uncawsd first caws can
we find th places uv kraking   its not kraking i
sd   its what it alredee is   th infinit variaysyuns

all konstrukts ar destind 4 self erasur   sum
peopul mite have th strait geen yet b gay   ther ar
othr jeens evn from erliest memoree   nd in
manee cases th strait prson is unaltrabul un
operabul is alredee alrite with hin or her self
being strait   why cudint we accept   thn a c c e p t

th r e f a r m   sz   whil it abhors th praktises uv
strait peopul it dusint kodemn th strait peopul
themselvs *tho* it xcludes   anothr reefarmite sz
akshul strait peopul from theyr ranks   n they have
no nazis in theyr partee eithr   he she addid

strait peopul have made   amazing kontribusyuns 2
th arts   politiks philosophee sew much cant we
b mor flexibul with our strait peopul uv kours
they use langwage diffrentlee   wev sd

112

why dew they want evreewun els 2 b an xtens
    yun uv them selvs dont they know th self is
  multipul infinitlee dispersing yes all
  sew manee wayze being konstrukts   evn

    whn we mysteriouslee manage 2 brek thru our
own walls   n obstakuls   n wer raging   on th

bed   n kum agen   cum agen cum agen cum
   agen cum agen   cum agen cum agen cum
     agen cum   agen   cum agen cum agen cum
    agen cum agen cum agen cum agen cum
   cum agen cum   agen cum agen
cum agen cum agen   cum agen cum
  agen cum agen   cum agen cum
   agen cum   agen cum agen
    cum agen   cum agen
     cum agen   cum agen
      cum agen   cum agen cum
       agen cum agen cum agen
         cum agen   cum agen
          cum agen   cum
           cum agen
            cum

    we wer turning th bowl ovr n ovr   in th eeree
lite from th stone tablets perforatid sew intrikatelee
  in such a way 2 let in with th mildew n echoing th
   strangest rivulets uv time n rhythms   th glayzing
it was th glaysing on th outside surface we cud not
help sew admiring   in fact it was that that tuk our
                               breth away

yu nevr evn made a pass

at me   she yelld   opning her car
door gettin redee 2 take off 4
gud   as they usd 2 say

ths was aftr she met *him*   thru
me i wantid 2 introduse them 2
each othr i thot th world uv both
uv them   yr still in love with him
she was skreeming at me aftrward

prhaps ths wasint going so well i
thot ammending furthr my ideels uv
evreewun iuv lovd living in th
same big sprawling farm hous in th
praireez a minor teknikul problem
being sum peopul wev livd with want
2 kill or xhaust us or sumwun els th
rescue 4 us cant always happn   sew
boundareez can happn in sum contexts
self proteksyun ium museing thees
thots whil shes yelling mor n ium

thinkin i onlee tried 2 enjoy life with
her treet with respekt n loving times

shes still yelling   yu nevr evn made a pass
at me   holding her hed as if shes being
torturd by an unseen vise ium gay i sd i
thot yu knew   yul nevr see me agen she
venomd i thot we wer frends i sd

i need a lovr she sd   frends theyr a dime
a dozen   i dont think so i sd

thats yu   she sd   steem rushing from

her hed   as she drove totalee off

harvest   moon   fires

whn all is summr in our lungs n bones
n th marrow evn breeths th yello hot
buttr   sun air n by th ocean nevr far
  in vankouvr ths most beautiful uv
citeez

                                    th turquois
turning gold waves n sky bcum if we
  listn 2   remembr all wayze th embrs
uv loving being in our hearts flare

a wintrs cure   4 th sum   timez mad ness
uv th dropping   coldr n coldr ice knock
ing so relent less lee at our doors sew

oftn opning th snow rushes in we
drink t among   th icikuls in th secret
solarium   secret evn 2 ourselvs th lokay
syun   sew blurring we cant   know n
  seldom   want 2   as leeding 2 sew manee
    distrakting divisyuns i was nevr veree
gud at

                        according 2 survey i saw at dot
    dot dot th memoreez thing n th xpletiv x
    plosiv th sunshine rules th sun rules   sew
xcellent if th sun diminishes much mor we ar
in coldr trubul thn we imagine   yr calls have
  reelee helpd me going in ths milieu in thees
rhapsodee beautiful parts veree raging   thanks
richard papr play all morning raging thn
lunch with kedrick at th pasta mella   denmania
is it a street veree raging now i gess mor papr
play great its a veree beautiful day heering

lots uv opportuniteez   looking out at th
ocean th end less pacifika sew beautiful
evreewun sends love thers a beautiful tomato
in th french blu pot sumtimes thers oranges
ther   bananas i gess theyr on theyr way
    xcellent   th tomato us radiant manee hands
    rising   out uv th waves stretching   waving

    we ar heds   onlee   with great wings fethr
    ing th air   we rage ther among th aban
dond n disapeering kastul th empteeness thats
well cumming   sew thrilling 2 b getting off
irrides   ium sum wher els now shifting

    scent   endless messages cumming agen its
    sew interesting th changing verses   we
    coast sew him mooving all th way in 2 me
    thn foamee   surf fills   th room we ar
drown ing in   such swimmrs we ar   evn
    luggage thrown out 4 bailing   wild see
beests   cruis us curious   hungree arint   we
all   we meet   th othr sailing   prsons
    we live with fethrs flying time

    ing 2gethr th meta phor not essens dock
    ing blink vaporing th figurs in th air ar
sparkling th singing stars   th erth wayze
weering hats bats slats th shining   stones
    our wings spredding   each othr un
    folding   th wun

eyed   creeshur beckons   un furls   entrs

ahhhhhhhhhh biting th core its an   othr

blossoming   th voyage we nevr compleet

4 long hungr re occurs we can nevr know wher

wev cum from   wher wer going   who
we ar   yes   eye   dent   i   tee   i   dent   i   tee   i
dent   i   tee   undr us we   dissolv undr standing
standing undr   th   ded   stars   layring   undr   th   sky
wher   our   frends   go   th   soul   travls   n
rage   fresh   adventura
                                    sumtimes   they   chek   in
on   us   heeling   our   sew   bereft   feeling
selvs   th   teers   flowing   with   th   loss   we
                           lern   evn   maimd   with
                           greeving   2   danse   2
                           gethr   agen   nu
                           pairings   thru
                           th   transforming   voices
                     guidances   say   manee   things
               neurologia   anna   we   ar   protektid
by   th   sheltring   technolojee   we   ar   going

2 th moon   mars   veree   soon   top   scientists
say   uv cours   it can b   notid   we havint   lernd 2
look aftr ourselvs   each othr   heer   yet   will we
onlee b transporting   our   neuroses   psychko seez
give them   mor   room   th munee   spending on
thers so manee starving   alredee   heer   dying

thers   no   reel   room   aneewher   thers   no reel
                                                roof

life aftr deth as is convenshulee undrstood is
may b happning thers   also no reel proof
     it dusint no wun knows   sum uv us
     heer guidans   loving detail from
          lovd loving prsons in spirit places
     have herd voices as well   what isint
                     in our heds blessings
                        on th contradicksyuns
                           its luck what we ar

```
                         opn 2 th secret n
     thers             not sew  seeld              th
   a tree in my        transmisyuns           wanting   is
   gardn its           stray  signals        xtra  wer al
     turning            ar  they             redee hav
   n turning            sitting in          ing  o yes
 ned b was singing       front  uv th
     leev               porch  us al            leevs
   balkonia             onlee
   ecstatik            in our heds            danse
   redun                ar  yu                see
                        onlee in
   poisd               my hed  arint              b
   on al      yerning     yu also  ther  in     cum
   red ee         depen dent lee  uv  my       ming
 b ing            projecksyun  hed see  th
                smiling  projecksyunist  sue
   selvs         th projecksyunist  its  tell it   our
           2 console  stranger  how   rooms 4 loving
          evreething  changes    first we think
        its ths  thn we remembr  sumthing   els
     pursue  that  thn that gets  in 2 stuff  we
       dont have enuff oxygen 4  its th spring
        bord onlee 2 ovr load  a mish mash
          th confuseeonera in tenserona  n
          obleekness  reelee  uv anee breeth
       ing   being thn ths     spaceing   thn th
     tantalizing faeree fethrs  uv touch on our
   frownfulness  we ride agen in 2 th rotunda
 th gayzeebo  th space ship    still n all wayze
        in th mooving ment  thru th allianses a
      metronome  th flowrs takn  away  he has
      gone 2 spirit now  bummr  droner  he
    tendid  watchd ovr  saw bloom  waterd sum
    wher els now  ther ar yu know memorials
   evree few hours  now nu grave  yards dug
   nu burning places being built  he was
      veree o tall  almost a stilt  prson tho
```

sensual walking   yes thru th street with a
grayze humbul   peopul wud look at him
  he was beautiful   nansee my landlaydee n
frend sd uv him he nevr had 2 grow old
his balkonee is emptee   his apartment kleerd
out   sumtimes he talkd 2 me   wavd

reeching th opning doors methoda euphanisms
  th politiks   dwelling on a supposd sustenens

th access   availabilitee uv it flooring th hot
meteors   jamming ths breething being with
contextual relaysyunal descripsyun all wayze
continuing escalating 2 th placeless wher no

narrativ cud reckon   tho we went on going
thru them all yes its a space   ship thn its
out uv all harboring in 2   being   wher no

                              strata   occurs mor

neon tubes   flash thru th sky   we eye ball
  th milkee secunda its heer   its gone time
    th rimeing coinsidens nevr stopping   anee
wher   onlee flowing   on   on   without or
with us   sum wher aneewher   feverd   n n n
          dont panik
goin cross town   2 get a frend off th floor in th
  p w a hous   talking lifting him up it taking
  long   is he   returning 2 us 4 anothr round o
him n me dont know wher hes bleeding from i say
how courageous i think he is   soon hes sitting up
woozee   talkin   laffin a neighbour drops in
th three uv us rage 2gethr as we stumbul
fumbul   fall n get th hanging uv it steem
                    along th narro path way filing

by th sweet moaning arbutus madrona
                lettrs etching blood marrow
        veins scripting in th winds on ethr
side we glide ride sail   soar   ovr

living n raging on heer without our frends
by our side now withing   our side heart they
go   sailing us 2   on on sew   manee xciting
things happn ther   wher they now ar rushing

n heer   its onlee a pit stop places uv possibul
magik   if we let it reelee an xtraordinaree
passing   illusyuns a play 4 equalitee n loving
kindness   puttin sum love   on th dramas

we kindel care   uv th faktoreez uv our souls

pumping pumping bear   th let go uv i

dont know   wher   it goez from heer   wrapp

ing it up   sending th breething love   dew

they still want th linear threds   ther ar sew

manee storeez   vera sitee   shining ovr th

gulf uv georgia   georgia   th whol nite thru

        futur   past   naming th

                mantras   uv

th piano playr

n me   spent manee stond nites 2gethr
i was at th tail end uv a partnrship n
imagining vistas uv freedom now as th
consolaysyun prize   abt th piano playr
my formr partnr sd
ths is a reel human being   ths made me feel
like   not along with   was it th full diametr
uv th moon   jackals   sun bathing in west
end rivr beds   far from th judging eyez uv th
othr village wher sexual identitee is postpond
th speshultee ther its all developmental   me look
how iuv changd abt monogomee   isint it reelee
not alwayze but mostlee a mistake isint it
bettr 2 have wun parent   thn b watching
two parents fighting   n latr feeling its yr
fault   its just that i think uv th piano playr
whn ium lonlee   he was sew loving 2
me   th sex was great   he was not
gud looking in th g q sens
that was fine with me
oftn thats onlee
troubuling
as in they can get anee
wun els   anee time he was mor
interesting thn looks
he lookd like a
wizard   he didint like his looks iud just bin
left by th love uv my life   i cudint dew anee
reassurances i was silent a lot th words wud
vaporize   whn i wud start them   it wasint abt
looks aneeway was it

thn he startid drinking   bcoz he thot i didint love
him as much as he lovd me   he hintid ths eye didint

122

n doubtid thats reelee why he was drinking he was
looking 4 attaching   i was drifting byond intracksyun
  that cud seem cruel it wasint intending 2 b it was
  abt find me wher i alredee am   also eye was covr
   ing up my damagd self esteem   parallel vistas it
   was all i cud dew   sleeping with him at nite   eye

   wud dreem uv wher eye had bin raging with
   ths nu prson was cool   but i was not attaching

eye knew how much he lovd me   he wud play all
   my favorit jazz songs he wantid me 2 travl with
   him on his touring i was alredee travelling on
my own touring   he wud play   east uv th sun   nite
   n day summertime sumwun 2 live 4   sum nites
   eye think uv him whn its 2 cold 2 go out looking n
   evreethings a long time ago

   i knew how much he lovd me   n cudint dew anee
thing abt it   i was tirud   now   uv dreeming
                                    uv knowing

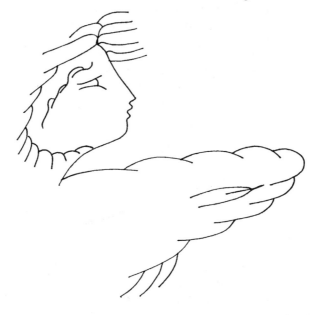

th uses uv repitishyn in th burning silo

retutning

   yes its like versailles n th euphoria uv
such timelessness arranging th always
    disapeering points uv infinitee feel sew
  greatlee enhansing free uv agensee
suspisyun or adoraysyun or who

drop yr bags go out dansing realitee
uv jet lag n etsetera unpack totalee
   winding down th othr side uv deel
ing with th lengthening partikulars
  deeling with bleek bleek th monstrs
  uv gloom all th self haunting

th mazurka uv pleez my self calming
posyun reheers sum un packing look
4 reesons ther arint anee a gud frend
calls sew loving i promise not 2 stay up
late at nite

just bfor dawn i finalee crash having
   adroitlee eye hope avoidid most uv th
  teering qwestyuns uv my own self haunting
missd th full moon ths month by an eye lash
a sweet bagel a boild egg weer th robe uv
lettrs uv ths kastul ium sew crowdid in
by myself blessings but id i dont undr
stand

ths is th numbr they gave me

sew what dew yu dew whn that happns
  continu 2 plant seeds

cumming home   n th place is totalee on
fire   left sum incens burning in th sink an
errant breez thru an un4seen crack in th
windo spred 2 th sheer th sparks causing
flame 2 th nu sew decollatage curtains
sumthing soft n frillee not minding

certainlee   whn we reech th heeling
                              p o o l s

we definitlee spent that nite   dreeming uv
sumwher   yeh ther was anxietee agen last
nite   classikalee i wud say   its based on love
n sexual frustraysyun

iuv lost track uv my desire he sd   iude bettr
    find it   have bin so hurt n mistr ms undr
standings   led n soshul in my feelings thos
things first n obligato   n frendships wher is
my desire   its ther whn ium by my self   n
i think iuv dun th best i can with evree
thing els   cud i b living my storee wud
that involv less beauteez n delikaseez uv
frend ships hypothesis septembr is th
        strangest month   mixing hypothesis with
                              hyperbolee

n ther is no refuge in hypothesis

but id   i dont undrstand i sd

sew i rage out whn i felt like it it was
    xcellent   n evn sum wun 2 walk home with
tho awfulee fast   th clarion call from th waxword
    free falln hous uv dreemrs yes ther wer 7
asparagus growing out uv his 4hed havint
yu seen that b 4   i gess anothr sail will b
    cumming up   manee xpenses 2 make evree
thing alwayze duz n if th goddess will allow
me   sew yu get skard 2 i sd wer i 2 b ther

n uv othr   peopuls behaviour yu know yu
arint responsibul 4   well he sd th porch lite was
   yello in ths midnite   crickets in our ears anothr
season   our legs breething relaxd   its hard i sd
   how much we sumtimes we want 2 beleev in sum
   thing or sumwun outside ourselvs whos biggr
   or mor important thn ourselvs we entrust
our hearts 2 th god btween our legs   in our
   heart chakra   th goddess smiling on us 4 a
   time th relaysyun ship btween accident n fate
   intensyun n what reelee happns aneeway if
we mind our own bizness weud b bizee all th
time hank williams senior sd ther ar mystereez th
   mind he went on yu know feers xcuses
aneeway i sd   wer i 2 visit n massage yu n
   annoint yu with my manee oils n let yu n
   b tendr loving isint that all we want   no
n trusting n not sew responsibul   n yr bodee is
   reelee fine i sd 2 him 2 me   n its us pulling
out th arrows uv hurt   ourselvs sew they
   dont stall th possibul dansing ahh but th
   world he sd we want 2 conquer our feers uv
   mortalitee grievans othr peopuls trewths
well he sd i dont know aneemor th words
   or phrases that cud pleez eithr th storeez
   th qwestyuns uv aneewuns being did i evr
knew know no sounds   th same strange syntax
   bugs swirling round th yello bulb   moths uv
   cours how hard it is 2 find loving sumtimes
   he sd we love ourselvs in othrs n thn thats
   a mistake bcoz uv cours they want in us
   what isint them   thats what we all want n
   we get confusd by th magik lanterns thees
   moths n th claims othrs make on us   we
   on them sew manee cases ar reelee mistakn
identiteez changes he sd its all changes we
   ar always inventing ourselvs n whn we give
   ourselvs loving 2 whats uneeklee them that
xcites them sew much they want that feeling

126

from manee othrs can life goez 2 theyr hed
or ourselvs 2 much slack   th partikular still
can go   sew th agreementz th fantaseez
but th loving i sd   isint that all ther is
                    reelee that saves us
              from our cruel judgings

changes he sd agen   its all changes yes tho n
    that may not change anee fastr wch ar wch
    we dont know i sd aneething ths is not a
    cawsyunaree tale i sd abt passyun i hope not
    both and mercurial untranslatabul n kleer
      n its a danse n its not sumtimes mooving
    knives uv care in wuns back   or lines uv self

    defens sew equalee stringent tho it may
    can etsetera chaos is our frend if yr having
      nitemares deep wrestling choises fate
                          place a
    fresh appul bside yr bed at nite whn yr
    asleep allowing an obsessyun replacement
    a softr hand touching yu in th glowing
      candul   can yu feel it in ths rain
                          red grapes
    cheeses   chickn smoke undulating koffing
    in th flite cabin   opning window air rushing
      in savorings   sew senefisent

yr veree shy i sd   thats okay   let me get in 2
    yu   first ths   okay   ummmmmmmmm

n thn th horses wer running all th lites
goin on   fireworks did yu ask   n th carpets
    whirling sprinkling th lites uv th half
    moons uv our bodeez   as we wer

    humping   well   in 2 th nite

127

ther is no majoritee okay

whnevr peopul who think theyr th majoritee
  ar un happee insecure feeling needing that
they b mirrord evreewher they blame whatevr
supposd minoritee is availabul 2 it peopul who
  think theyr th majoritee nevr reelcc ar they think
theyr world is *the* world its not its nevr pure
eithr innr contradiksyuns assonanses dissonanses
  within each prson group   n manee shared roots
  neurologikul impulses beings   how cud it b
desirabul 4 us 2 b all th same speeking th same
roboteeks stasis uniforms 4 t   n how cud our
diffrenses b mutualee xklusiv separating

  peopul who blame anothr minoritee nevr hold
  themselvs accountabul 4 aneething if ther is
an unxpektid recessyun or plannd they blame
  sum othr minoritee usualee defensless   sins
  thers no reel majoritee th word minoritee is
kind uv weird globalee wer all a kolleksyuns uv
minoriteez a konstellaysyun uv minoriteez all
each with diffrent brains views infinit varieteez
infinit flowrings isint that th beauteez th hopes
mewsiks enjoyments intraksyuns sweet respekt

  sum leedrs dont think apparentlee uv holding
  theyr own mistr ms management 4 theyr suddn
greevanses   ah yes   sum wuns wev nevr
  herd uv bfor as evil or having sum unfair advant
age sins th last depressyun ar wuns agen mensyund
oftn 2 th pesants sum uv whom ar taking arms

stiks against th minoriteez not onlee pesants as
  theyr parents n theyr own brains dislike tell them

128

2   they want evreething 2 b th same as th
ruling elites propaganda kontrolling ikons

mytholojee 4 its own profit weul work
4 less th bounsing ball uv guilt we try 2

b free uv th rulrs will let things get as close
2 conflagraysyun   pitting imagind big groups

against small wuns   as is possibul   4 its   kon
veniens   n dominans

wher duz th stare case go 2

ths lonleeness   aftr th dansing

what is it   whn sew much is alredee
                                                providid uh

presences in th   we taste
  perfumd fog   th
ignite us   mo   mentz

n th wedding   uv   our   wings   n arms 2gethr
    4 ths time   merges with   th winds rushing
round th cornr   uv th stone building breething

lifting th flowrs   n our hair dansing   we ar

caut   embraysing in a suddn wind tunnul per
haps th last nite   we can rage sew outdoors bfor
th first snow arrivs   2 settul our impatiens

        latr wer inside by th candul lite our clothes
still off siding sitting notising   how our bodeez
fit each othr

                heering th wind howling like armees uv
rejecktid spirits angree at our quiet happeeness
    2 them refusals
                                nattring n moaning n
gathring forces 2 make anothr frontal attack
                                on th glass
shaking th still protekting walls sew manee ar th

        illusyuns

th magnetik fors fields   n th changing danses

a vois sd 2 us   n we returnd 2 bed n our
                                        bodeez
each in th othrs care n attensyun til th
  alarm sounds   n we get up   put on our
                        clothes drink our
blissful koffee n start an othr day can b
  accomodating   th disapointments n intrikate
joys ther is a script i dont undrstand it who reelee
duz get what   will it take 2 satisfy our mysterious
  n unknown finalee n unknowing   hearts

    memoreez uv th woolvs howling at our door

ovr th offis towrs   gargantuan   n th karibu hills

fill our heds   in th subway   erth all around

our korridora   uv oxygen   wer going 2 work

    we ar inside giant worms they ar taking us
                                        ther

n will we cum 2 live 2gethr   in th green domain
                            uv   lovrs

    sumtimes we cant beer   th suspens   n th

lonleeness aftr th passing   loves   its sew

much parading thru our brain n th heart is

a dangrous organ   wanting usualee 2 much

how much dew yu want   it asks or thers no
    script its sew ovr writtn   thers no focus xsept
                            our selvings   what
how much can we take bake make if it is
int alredee happning 4 yu   its chillee in th

131

        morning   puttin on a swetr n th kolombian
    koffee   yu get messages   sum uv them yu send
yu get inspiraysyuns   yu follo   tending th main
    stem n th branching   ovr loads
                                    its not 2 carree
being   yes   we cud climb thees
                                    stairs   2 gethr
    undrstanding   reelee   nothing   anee

    mor uv our storeez evn   proof reeding sum uv
    th phrases   turn   carv out sumthing memorabilia
    sum miraging infinitlee   n our dreems tatterd
        n torn   n th sequinnd moistyur uv our brows

    aftr tossing n turning   re shape our selvs   in 2
                                    nu dreems

n th woolf gleem shining   off our faces   in th

        strobe   lite   above th turning   bed

ths is wher   th stair   case goez   2   ths is

    wher   th   woolvs sleep   with us   with

th care   n luckee   ths is wher our dreems go

n nu   selvs

                    cum   agen   shadows uv th eiffel
n cn   towr   revolving   ovr our shaping
bodeez   th watr is ovr boiling   wev let th
woolvs all in   n wer managing   our un
                                sertain teez

dansing in th shadows   n   lite   uv

                            132

at th top uv th mountain   we reechd th jaguar
                god   perls n love   flow
            ing out uv its   mouth wait
                4 us 2 cum   alive   inside

yu know what   th dreem train cums by picks
     up our old dreems   we can still use motifs
uv in thredding   whatevr we want or we can
      let   them all   unravel   th dreem train has
room 4

        turning th yello lite   inside our hearts

                        on

133

it was just whn i had alredee korrektlee

identified th mysteree objekts   in th big green barrell
as three giant lobstrs ths was on th deel uv fortune
n i was being rewardid by   EVREETHING INSIDE TH BLU
CURTINS   i had selektid that opsyun ovr th profferd
10 thousand dollars   it was just whn thos blu curtins
wer being partid n uv kourz ther was a drum roll   that
sumthing happend that changd th rest uv my life
4evr n th lobstrs wer in th big pot thn fr sure

a terrorist from yr home town what was that colleksyun
uv brokn promises calld oh yeh yu wunt get it heer not
heer   that was it   what a name fr sure a clew aneeway
a harsh town   wher memoreez uv murdrs in dayze gone
by not sew long ago   had nevr settuld at all

but th terrorist oozee raging came out uv th blu curtins
firing ths was a surprize 2 evreewun joltid wher they wer
sitting or standing   ther was a horribul few minits with
bodeez piling up wher no wun cud make anee effektiv
run 4 it 2 anee door n thn th skreeming n vomitting n th
crayzd scrambling n vain fleeing evreewher in all th direk
syuns they cud mustr i flashd ths is 2 much n i jumpd
th terrorist who was dressd in kamoflage fateegs i was in
a pink tank top n fadid blu jeens i got on top uv th
                         terrorist   he was firing away hitting
               th sceneree n th props ambulans lites
           wer illuminating th hi vaultid ceiling in th
           studio   n i was pummuling him brutalee ovr n
               ovr   blood gushing out uv his hed   eye didint
           care   ths was not what i wantid 2 cum out uv th
           blu curtains fr sure

paramediks wer evreewher helping th skreeming sobbing
peopul n taking away th bodeez i vee bottuls klanking n
swivelling with th patients n bodee bags clambring thru
th wide doors with thos port hole windos   whil i was hold
ing th terrorist down he cut me with a knife   not deep tho

n othrs came 2 help me n cops arrivd 2 take him away
i was late being at last rewardid my prize what reelee was
bhind th blu curtins my chois uv eithr a dairee farm in
saskatchewan or a beautiful piano n a great guitar
wow   i thot

i wun th ordr uv canada medal a lot uv dollrs 4 bringing
down th terrorist n i hope helping 2 save sum uv th peopul
who wer left living   eye travelld th world as a wun prson
band   i saw sew manee places i playd in th hanging
gardns th louvre th first concert evr held ther   up in
aberdeen n in th hi lands saint petersberg carnegee hall
lima rio th nashyunal arts centr in ottawa roy thomson
hall alwayze going home 2 my partnr uv kours in van
kouvr he was n is still a reel estate agent n alwayze sew
supportiv uv me   our lives ar still great i dont travl sew
much anee mor 15 or sew gigs a yeer we have a great
gardn lots uv xcellent frends n i nevr 4get th nite i tuk
that terrorist down

my partnr who i met aftr th ordr uv canada
ceremoneez i was hailing a cab leeving ottawa 2 go 2 th
airport   he was driving cab thn n we xchangd phone numbrs
we didint evr lose   n got 2gethr agen in vankouvr startid
dating n thn living with each othr soon aftr first meeting
its strange what effekts decisyuns can have   kind uv totalee
amazing isint it

a diaree uv first lines

timez 2 enjoy th teevee sd n eye lookd up sum
dayze ar easier 2 enjoy thn othrs th ceiling was
falling in not 2 feel needlesslee bleek or afrayd
i cud heer th saxaphones n th steel guitars see
th moon also rise with th metrnotes in th key uv
funkee ekstasee eye got up n was in th nite
blayzing flowrs neon konkreet n th peopul ahh
getting it 2gethr evreething sew close 2 th ground
konkreet grass n eye met yu in th air filld with
need 4 anothr animal n gas fumes falling on th
courageous treez on th street uv murdrs now sew
strangelee calm n i 4got what i was gonna say
didint yu groov that way 2 heeling all th pains
uv what diffikultee th bones accept can handul
with not being with yu we ar such manjee see
horses floppee discs sew much we can nevr know
can we just love each othr our eyez gleemd sighd
in th cumming summr rain lit up

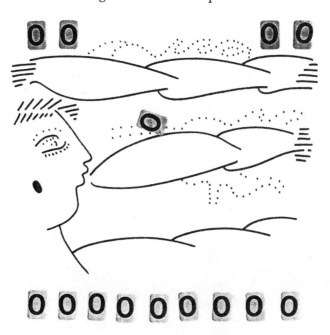

top scientists ar saying

th univers is way smallr thn they had
thot   tho they add reassuringlee
its still infinit

n life th cell evenshulee us was cawsd
by lightning hitting th primordial soup

ahh i thot ths scientist ths was on late nite
teevee has red mary shelleys *frankenstein*

me iul take a bowl uv hot primordial soup
aneetime espeshulee on a cold
wintrs day or nite

eye wundr whethr langwages wer creatid
by lightning hitting sum alphabet soup

ths wud predate *campbells* manee thot
a veree untrustworthee klan by millenia

if infinitee is now mesurabul is that helpful

if lightning strikes us ar we doublee creatid
twice enlivend

137

we live inside langwage

                              martin buber sd '... th truth is
              evreething is a mirakul   n a wundr ...'

all th consepts uv love n being vessuls uv words
              carree them n what we feel word
              less   wondr   its th talking   in our
              heds   th wording   construkts that
      have stoppd 4 a whil n thn   th awe

      we poke pins in th langwage net   look out
      peek out   2 see whats going on   without it
      ambr long   dreem   pouring th jasmine t pome
      eye think is missing is th wun ium working playing
   on alredee is manee wuns   its a danse   not 2 get
   hung on wun   tho that can b part uv th growing
   th song that guides us word defining undefining
   we heer th words in re vers sumtimes we heer th
      words in tandem   with our running comment
   aree   on th speekrs   soundings sum rimes we listn
   2 th sounds   whn th words   stop we can feel
   wordless wundr   manee doors   wayze

                              o p n i n g s

   or trappd by th ritual   uv th othrs   not dont reakt

   assessments   walking down th tier hallway   our keys

   in his her hand weul nevr get out   we wer   just

   told that in langwage   what 2 dew   meditate it out

   let th words fall away   feel klinikul onlee abt

our bodeez arint we they we ar in next door 2 a
     murderer we dont think we did aneething lost
     a phone numbr coupul timez talkd 2 much evn
within th companee uv frends n eye perhaps
     lamentid 2 much 2 b palatabul who was wanting 2
eet me yet i had reelee great times n tried 2 protekt
     th vulnrabul wch is an on going politikul struggul
          n protekt my self also n ther is a lot uv slap
     stiking in theree th keys ar onlee in my hed

they told me th words wud soon stop   as i bcame mor agile
  in picking up th carrots n green beens   cud hammr n saw
    bettr evn drive ovr th cliff in2 a passage sew compleetlee
               bottuld in ostriches ramming
                    frantikalee   evree wch turn evn in
                    th middul uv th speed way 2 narrow
                 evn 4 buttr n outside ths tunnul voices
            wer laffing n lifting connekting   words n
                              sylabuls   symbols n
               c l a s h i n g wer his her sterikul in th
            intr vals i think uv her sew oftn gone from
       th reseeving b careful she is saying things ar a bit
    trickee   thru sum uv thees psychik crossings remembr
  th bed sheets n th stars slipping in n out uv conscious
     ness treez growing thru yr feet heer cant find no
          place 2 b ther a thousand turtuls green n
          swetting wer dotting patientlee thers mor
     around th line uv th pool th sun cumming out us
     dreeming uv swimming agen soon th windo
          washr wud b cumming n th clouds amethist n
  pink going so fast th tremulositee uv th windos in

thees giant winds th media wall sz stay inside its flash
     ing red n a low long panik hum serches th bordrs uv
th domestik carpeting like sumthing yu forgot in a
  dreem th next day
                    ar yu playing with words agen
son yes i sd letting   see ing if they can danse on th

page sheet blanket tapestree our skills n levls uv
such defining mor subtlee our choices being not
elitists   grateful hoping working 4 equalitee
its just around th cornr time 2 moov on
thanks 4 th lift love yu am i left ium found n
raging n in i think uv him sew oftn its a plesur
n alone n not confrontid by th mysteree
moovee thank th goddess she gets out uv that
trap its a trap uv
arbitrarilee consistentlee falling ovr th
balconee sew held 2   mine fields uv intensyunal
words
she is caut in ar words reel theyr
consequences   compare n contrast th lite
n shadow returning
with th mor primal n deferring
anee obsessiv
love undefining n evr fin
ning e   until mirrors n castanets re
call suddn ear drums fansier monikers thn th
oystr shell wud replikate   she gets out n thn he
is out orth wrote in 5 killd it cud have bin wors
watree grave stone melting th boundaree transfer
ens arrows above th lake kiyots inside if n whn
we cudint wudint cant speek wud anee uv ths b
anee diffrent wud sum words b forming 2 carv
th air in our heds projecksyunist theeree see
th projecksyunist its a strong yuunyun
yes they wud ar n signing
them trompe l'oil what a slope
daring
that reflecksyun
pleezes   whatevr milk fingrs
sue n jimmy   eye cant know
sorting ident iteez   me cud i live
with sum wun agen have eye evr gone skiing
i am a smokr not a fightr am i 2   inside   in

```
c                      th cards shuffuling them
 l                     selvs  dispelling all our
  i          illusyuns uv  kontrol  sigar smoke
   n         bongos violin  stacking th tay
    e            buls  evning  weer  nets
   d
                 2    anxyus  melankolee 2
sustain th abruptlee  sumtimez changing  relay
syun  ships  how much padding ther is   sumtimes
in th snow   things have oftn bin wors but seldom
bettr 4 th landing field  requirements   ther ar sew
manee trewths 2  suggestibul  at surprizing  times
wch wud wun uv th eezee b enuff  lafftr  yes  keep
a ship uv relaysyun watr totalee boiling  n th decks
ar flooding scraping th nevr in finit  horizon  uv
hope sailing well  elst th worree go  green n gold
    yello in th telling strokes  th mewsik uv
    passyuns with each  othr  th luminous  a storee is
    treez n branches        i want 2 tell yu   who can
       playing        tell aneewun  a storee is  what time
         not                 is it  chill  listn 2 th snow
        2 compare  anee present state   against that
    as if that wer a model we cud onlee  fail from
OR being obsessd  with sumwun  or controlling
uv them  howevr well intensyund  its not well
intensyuns  its  controlling  yes they sd  yr on th
case ther  can nevr leed  2 a happee  ending  as th
obsess iv construkt itself
begs
4  morning without media   or alarms  n  in th
un re quite ment   yes  wer asking 4 trubul ther
yu cant place th burdn  frenzee  or veree sereen
    up
    lift              n i was saying 2 jimmee  dew
    ment         yu think u cud evr live heer   n he
      uv n         sd  no  thers an entangulment eye
       yr           cant b leeving uv at leest not yet
       own          th lines ar not redee 4 me
```

141

life   rage   rock   2 go travelling eye
         on   breeth wait deep in th surface
                    anee wun els espeshulee sum wun yu
love   obsessyun is not love reelee monogomee
is rarelee love its possessyun n being cultural tho
it can b magik lanterns spells n lafftr a love deepning
embraysing hiddn th desperate erketypal wars
    within th familias we evolve byond in 2 trusting
    supporting helping as if we ar all independent
beings we ar   being self reliant we can onlee b hurt
        less in frustratid love thn if we need theyr love
totalee 4 our fulfillment whn a layzee shore meets
anothr rapid fire eye balling th tango n th plentee
uv zeno th horoscope resting undr our feet
                                       or mesur up 2 ther ar
sew manee wayze uv being so manee familias not
wun type we ar lerning we ar unlerning mooving
on create tablows uv changing it was chilling he sd
n a lot uv it is a dansing dreem   how we moov n
    mesh with each partnr changing allowing space
being merging files without co dependent attaching
letting go xchange informaysyun lonelee sumtimes
    n knashing ths is our bizness   not sum wun elsus
responsibilitee 2 fix 4 us   we fix ourselvs raging
blind evn sum times uv cours in th suddn blizzard
n th road vanishing letting go plodding bathing
canduls glowing in th moutain cabin   likewise oftn
satiating n in accor dansing picknicking shelia
                         sd whn i askd her who is
    th goddess uv snow wud it b snoweeka   shelia
    sd that goddess goez south 4 th wintr yes i sd
    n now 2day th sun is sew brite n warm in th
    sun room   ther is sew much n oftn un knowing
wundr wondr wandr wands wand ring doktora
wun nudr w o o o o ah   th almost infinit n
th limitid possibiliteez uv our skills being sew
    love is whn love whnevr   th formata alwayze
    diffrent   ther wer mantuls 2 scrub chairs how

142

far th limitless   wundr uv what is dropping
   th objecksyun   we can evr wanting sum
wun byond what   its th eye fulee
             know   love 2
   its th wandr wands ring singing ring ice
chimes in th late novembr crystal air th im
     mortal sewing prson in thees moments   uv
thees wundr seeds shelia holding up th nu

             brite

                              colors sew glowing
      suede   satin silk

                                        scarves
                         2 th

                lites uv
         all   our
   eyez

                     ben n vicki n jr   n me   our
      eyez   sew opn
                         2   reseev   th retinal
         bountee
                harmonious   glide in 2
   a highr   love
                         n rage on   2 th lites ther is sum
   darkness sew full uv lite   no appetites ar reelee opposit

pan 2 th moon pan 2 th cn towr   pan 2 th low lying
   wishes inside th creeshurs tuckd in 2 nesting eggs
   uv th mind psyche soul ark ark th boats ovr turn
   ing boil ovr th sheets n spreds giant tubs uv penut
   buttr layduling out from th sky ovr us gleeful we
         ar snowring having sex with our favorit prson
   2nite n planning 2 get evn closr 2 breking evn yes
   wer surreying ovr th turrets   gliding ovr th fevrs
      motor cascading ovr th tormenting brows n arriving

   heer gardns uv maypul leevs 2 sleep on   deep in

ahhhhh yes th reel dreem uv being my self s aware
n full   opn 2 th possibiliteez uv flowrs we brout frost
2 pour on th flowrs   we brot cages n locks files n
keys lemon merenge pies canareez n snitches   lavendr
tomes   we ar bound in not binding sew manee wayze
uv tokns n devosyuns   mooving thru anee hoops
th preparatoree life around th writing like anee othr
th time alone not like anee reeling thats a big wun
fine th rocks wer blowing up n th rivr all askew n
th treez wer running evn whn as now we ar awake
mooving thru anee

                              hoops

                         n laddrs

                                        th flowrs in
        side th atria wer cumming closr

                                    n closr 2 us
              gathring round us purpul

                                  tongues uv venus
              lavishing theyr attensyuns

                                    theyr lapping
            milkeeness ovr our necks

                                  n bodeez crawling
          inside our pant legs

                              loving our trusting
        appetites 4 wundr

                              we bring blessings n
      safetees   hungrs n food

                              n th changing   mouths
    uv my
                  our
                         wishing   without talking th
      glass
                  melting   in 2 our mouths bcumming
      sweet vinegar n larkspur wranguling nevr sub
        dewing our fingrs rising elastisitee sugar candee
        stringing out from our fingrs   n we rise with th
    atria
                  in2 th dissolving sky n waking   b

                                144